WENDY KREMER

I'LL BE
WAITING

Complete and Unabridged

LINFORD
Leicester

First published in Great Britain in 2010

First Linford Edition
published 2012

British Library CIP Data

Kremer, Wendy.
  I'll be waiting.- -(Linford romance library)
  1. Love stories.
  2. Large type books.
  I. Title II. Series
  823.9'2–dc23

  ISBN 978–1–4448–0994–7

Published by
F. A. Thorpe (Publishing)
Anstey, Leicestershire
Set by Words & Graphics Ltd.
Anstey, Leicestershire
Printed and bound in Great Britain by
T. J. International Ltd., Padstow, Cornwall

This book is printed on acid-free paper

I'LL BE WAITING

Jill's job is selling houses or office complexes, but now she's challenged to find new owners for a small rugged island. Until now the National Trust leased the island and its warden, Blake, wants it to stay that way. Blake's colleague, Sharon, longs to be his girl, but Jill is attracted to Blake too — until she believes he's manipulating their friendship for his own ends. So, in finding a buyer, will the cost to Jill be a broken heart?

1

Jill Douglas looked critically at the company's finished advertisement on the computer screen. *Buy your own island! Guaranteed sea views — and no neighbours.*

She thought about her current day-to-day hectic life; about trying to persuade prospective buyers that a property they weren't interested in, was worth a closer look. A life on a secluded, remote island seemed a wonderful idea. This one was up for sale, and it was her fate to sell it to someone.

Her initial romantic interest plummeted sharply, however, as she read the text through to the end. She printed out the details, and with the papers filed neatly in an orange folder, glanced through the half-glass partition between the two small offices and saw that her boss, John, was free.

She tucked her shoulder-length ash-blonde hair tidily behind her ears and took a moment to straighten her skirt before she went in. John liked his employees to look well turned-out, and she didn't want to give him chance to pass one of his nonsensical comments this morning. In his way, John was a love — but he did tend to go on and on.

She held the folder aloft and gestured with it in his direction. 'John — this island you've taken on is a pretty hard nut to crack, you realise that, I hope?'

John waved his ringed hands in the air impatiently. Vaguely he reminded her of Karl Lagerfeld — only Karl Lagerfeld was thinner, and considerably more intelligent. 'Nuts were created by God for a good reason, Jill. In this case, we are nutcrackers. Just think of your share of the commission when you sell it, my darling!'

Jill could only think about the fact that she was ordained to be the nutcracker, not John. It was easy for him to press his fingertips together, and act so blasé. She tilted her head and continued, calm but insistent.

'Have you seen the details that came in with it — the ones Clive included in the advert? This is not a palm-fringed paradise with sandy beaches and translucent seas! It's only accessible by boat, apart from a very short time at low tide. From the pictures, I wouldn't be surprised if the jetty was rotten; it looks like it. Did you happen to notice this island is also a Site of Special Scientific Interest? Whoever buys it, for whatever reason, will always be under close scrutiny, and I suspect building permission to put up any kind of structures will be null.

'I'm sure the description 'uninhabited and up for sale for the first time in two generations' might sound very enticing to a starry-eyed, moneyed, prospective buyer who hasn't seen the actual site, but I'm the one who has to point out that they require waders and waterproof clothing before I can even take them on a viewing.'

'Oh, Jill! You have been selling houses too long. You are so fault-finding and such a cynic! Moreover, you are wrong. There is a house on the island; a fine stone Victorian pile, or so it seems — even if it hasn't been lived in for years. Somewhere in this world, someone is longing to own this gem. I'm sure they'll be able to have a ding-dong in flip-flops and swimming costumes in the summertime.'

Jill raised her eyebrows. 'Really?'

'Think of it as the ultimate challenge! You are the perfect choice for a demanding task like this. You love the outdoors — and you don't even mind wearing wellies.' He studied his manicured nails and then looked up at his assistant. 'Although I can't imagine why anyone on this planet would want to — they're so inelegant and ugly! But — ' he smiled encouragingly ' — you're an intrepid soul, an open-air freak, and you come from a rural background. You're absolutely ideal to flog this place!'

Jill glared. 'Just because I'm from a farming family and can drive a tractor, doesn't mean that I actually want to spend my working hours up to my knees in mud.'

'That's understandable, but it's on our books now, darling. We have to try to shift it.' John moved uneasily in his comfortable leather chair. 'You have nothing special on schedule at present. Take a day or two; go and take a look at the place yourself. I'm sure you'll be able to find some agreeable aspects you can incorporate into your chitchat by the time you come back.'

* * *

Jill was doing just that now. She shoved her hands deeper into the pockets of her weatherproofs and buried her chin in her collar as she surveyed the island from some mud flats opposite. There was a steady, cold wind blowing inwards from the direction of the grey sea beyond. She bore in mind that it was for sale for £100,000 — and finding someone who might be interested in it at this time of year wasn't a likely prospect. Perhaps an advert in some of the London newspapers around Christmastime might be worth the outlay?

From her present vantage point, she could make out straggly trees, bushes and grey rocks along the shoreline. The shore was bordered with reeds and depressing mud banks, which merged with the dull grey seawater. The fourteen-acre island still managed to look quite impressive from a distance. She noticed that the water further up the four-hundred-metre wide channel between land and the island was swirling fiercely around a group of rocks. Gill presumed the island might be a tricky place for a boat to land if the jetty was damaged. Apart from a patch of pebbles and shingle, where the jetty projected into the land, she couldn't see anywhere else that might be suitable. She'd have to find out the times of low tides, and if it was feasible to walk across safely.

Except for the occasional calls of birds, all was silent around her. She took a digital camera out of her shoulder bag and took a few pictures before returning thankfully to her red Mini. It had rained heavily in the night and her second-best suede boots were soaked with rain. Consulting a map, she found there was a small village nearby. She decided to find a pub, and ask where she could find accommodation for the night.

She found it, ten minutes further along the main road. It was typical for the area; red-bricked houses and windswept gardens. The hill behind the village was covered in thickly clustered pines, and on the opposite side was a monotonous rolling landscape only broken up here and there with dried-out grasses, protruding rocks and bedraggled bushes. Halfway along the wandering village street was a tidy-looking small pub with a white porch; the ivy growing up its walls was waving angrily in the wind.

Stepping inside, Jill almost whooped at the sight of a fire burning in an open fireplace. A grandfather clock ticked majestically in the corner, a well-polished, well-stocked bar took up most of one wall, and the furniture was welcoming. For a moment the room was empty, but a door behind the bar opened as Jill walked toward the counter. A pleasant-looking middle-aged woman with grey eyes and grey wavy hair gave her a welcoming smile.

'Afternoon! Something to drink?'

Jill unbuttoned her coat and folded it over the back of a nearby chair. 'Thanks! A vodka and lemon, please.' She shook her hair and looked around. 'I'm looking for somewhere to stay the night. Can you recommend somewhere locally?' She picked up the glass and made herself comfortable on the leather bar stool.

The landlady smiled. 'There aren't many hotels hereabout, but we have a couple of rooms we let out to tourists. Will that suit? In the summer, hikers pass back and fore when they're following the coastal path, or visiting the nature reserve. Some want to stay overnight. In winter it's a lot quieter around here.'

Jill smiled. 'It sounds perfect! Is there a chance of an evening meal too?'

The woman nodded. 'I'm Mary Owen; my husband Don and I run the pub. We have plain, hearty meals — as long as you don't expect anything fancy, you're very welcome!'

'I'm Jill Douglas, and I'm sure I'll love your cooking.'

'Well, finish your drink in peace, and then I'll show you the room. I always keep it ready and waiting, but I'll just pop up and turn the heating up, so that it'll be nice and cosy for you.' She disappeared.

Jill took her drink and went to sit by the inglenook fireplace. She stretched her long legs out straight, settled her slender figure in a comfortable position, ruffled her damp hair and thanked Heaven that she'd already found somewhere so easily.

The woman returned and came over to the corner to chat. 'Passing through? We don't see many people at this time of year.'

Jill didn't see any reason not to lay her cards on the table. 'I came to see Coomer Island. My firm has been commissioned to sell it.'

The landlady's eyes widened. 'Someone mentioned they'd heard it was up for sale, but I didn't think things were so far along.'

'I haven't been across yet. I just looked from the banking. I'll have to get myself a table of the tides and find someone who can take me across tomorrow. There's a house on the island, isn't there?'

Mrs Owen nodded. 'No one has lived there for at least ten years. When Mrs Barry's husband died, she stuck it out alone for many years, until just before she died. We often thought it must have been a very lonely life over there on her own, but she didn't seem to mind. She had two children, but as far as I know one lives in Sussex and the other in Devon somewhere. They rarely visited their mother. I wouldn't recognise one of them if they walked through the door this minute!' She crossed her arms over her chest. 'Jack Lewis has an aluminium boat; he'll probably ferry you across if you ask him.'

'Where do I find him?'

'Sometimes he comes in for a pint; if he doesn't call this evening, it's still easy to find him. He and his wife live in the first cottage on the main road after you leave the village. I thought the conservation body had leased out the island from the owners, because of the ducks and geese and things over there.'

Secretly, Jill was feeling pleased; she hadn't reckoned it would be so simple to find someone to take her across. She nodded and took a sip of her drink. 'Up until now, it was. It looks as though the family have finally decided they are never going to use it and have made up their minds to sell. It's the most sensible thing for them to do, if they don't intend to visit or make use of it in some way in the future.'

Mrs Owens brows wrinkled. 'Blake won't like it.'

'Blake? Who's he?'

'Blake is chief warden of the nature conservation centre. A very nice chap. He calls from time to time for a pint and a chat; always polite.'

Jill shrugged. 'I'm afraid I can't help it if he doesn't approve. Perhaps no one will be interested — then the family will probably be glad to extend the lease to the conservation people. It's due to run out in six months' time.'

'It won't make a lot of difference to us in the village, if the island is sold or not,' Mrs Owen mused. 'It won't bring any more money to the village. We don't have a grocery shop or a baker's or such any more. A van comes round once a week with some essentials, and people fetch the rest from the supermarket on the edge of the next big town.' She smiled. 'If you're ready I'll take you upstairs.'

Jill jumped to her feet and gulped the last of her drink. 'I'll get my overnight bag from my car.'

'You can park that round the back, and come in through the back entrance. Your meal will be waiting in an hour's time. You can eat here in the bar or in your room, if you prefer.'

'I'll come to the bar. Thanks, Mrs Owen!'

The older woman smiled 'You're welcome, my dear.'

* * *

Jack Lewis ran a hand over his weathered face, and regarded her with a sceptical expression.

Jill hurried to reassure him. 'I don't mind getting wet or muddy, honestly! Look, I'm dressed very sensibly; windproof jacket, thick woollen jumper, warm jeans tucked into wellingtons, gloves, a warm scarf and a bobble — hat!' She didn't mention she was also wearing thermal underwear — she hadn't grown up on a farm not to know how to dress for a cold offshore trip.

'Well, okay! This is a funny time of the year to go exploring over there.'

Jill nodded. 'Yes, I know; it's a bit mad, isn't it, but it's part of my job to check the properties we're trying to sell. If I can't see things for myself, I don't know what to praise, or what to warn someone else about.'

'Humph! Funny way to earn a living if you ask me. Hang on, I'll just get my coat and tell the wife where I've gone.'

Once in his boat, Jack let the vessel drift downstream. When the current grew weaker, he headed out to sea, then turned back to run parallel with the island on its seaward side. 'It's easier to go with the flow than to fight the strong currents in the channel,' he explained. 'Takes less fuel, too.'

Jill nodded and spoke loudly because

of the wind and the sound of the engine. 'So you come in to the jetty from the top end of the island?'

'Yep! You got it.'

'Isn't there a place to land on the opposite side?'

His deep-set wrinkled eyes looked confidently out to sea. 'No. There's a nice little cove on that part, but there are a lot of hidden rocks that will rip the bottom out of a boat if you try to beach that way.'

Jill took photos as they followed the outline of the land. She spotted the cove Jack had mentioned, and it looked inviting. Even now in the early winter, and from this distance, she could imagine it would be a lovely place to idle the day away, if the weather was warm enough. She tightened her scarf around her neck. There were some positive features to this assignment after all. They rounded the top end and Jack let the current carry them down towards the jetty. He used the engine to keep them on course, and Jill was soon scrambling out onto the wooden planking. She noticed it had been repaired in places with newer pieces of wood, so it wasn't the rotten construction she'd expected after all. Her mood improved.

'Thanks, Jack!'

He touched the peak of his cap. 'Sure you'll be all right on your own?'

'You said low tide is just before three, and it's quite safe to walk back then, is that right? That gives me two and a half hours to look around. That's plenty of time.'

He nodded. 'The walkway is fairly firm underfoot, because of the rocky foundations. You're not likely to even get wet feet if you watch the time and take care. It takes about ten minutes to walk back to our place, once you're on solid ground again.'

'I'll let you know I've survived when I come for my car. How much do I owe you?'

He rebuffed her offer, holding up his hands. 'It's okay. If it was a regular thing I'd take money, but a one-off like this is on the house!' He revved the engine, pushed away from the jetty and used the current to join the flow of the water. In a matter of minutes, he was out of sight and Jill was alone with the sounds of Coomer Island.

She followed a well-trodden footpath. Nettles were growing abundantly everywhere. The way twisted and turned down the damp track that was bordered with overgrown hawthorn bushes and other vegetation. She emerged in front of a broad stretch of green that wasn't so overgrown and sloped slightly upwards. Looking at it, she mused that it might even have been a cultivated lawn at one time. She walked towards a solid-looking grey stone house with a covered stained-glass entrance porch.

To her surprise, the house looked quite pretty, and it still appeared to be in good condition, although the paintwork was dried and peeling. She tried the door, but it was locked. She made do with stealing a look at the living room through a grimy window framed by washed-out curtains. She could make out sagging armchairs with faded covers, some heavy Victorian furniture, dull carpets and an old-fashioned lamp standing in a corner behind the door. At least everything looked dry. The kitchen had some old-fashioned equipment and looked just as shabby and neglected as the rest. She longed to see the rest of the interior but, short of breaking in through one of the windows, there was no way of doing so.

Round the back was a small outhouse. The door was hanging on its hinges; inside were some archaic-looking gardening tools, and the usual kind of rubbish that collected in any garden shed.

Jill took some photos, and continued on her way; trying to explore the island's periphery as far as that was possible. She had to scramble over obstacles, avoiding untamed vegetation, ruts and puddles. Now and then, there were welcome gaps between the trees and bushes.

The vegetation seemed thicker nearer the shore than towards the centre. Making constant detours, she spent an hour wandering, and then returned to the house. She remembered to watch the time and finally strolled downhill, via a well-worn pathway behind the house, to the small cove she'd noticed from Jack's boat. Some weak rays of sun were struggling out from behind the clouds.

Jill sat down, ate part of a chocolate bar she had in her pocket and leaned back. She stretched her legs out along the surface of the rough rock, closed her eyes to enjoy the smooth melting taste in her mouth and took pleasure in the moment of peace. There was a lovely stillness to the place, only interrupted by the calls of various birds hidden somewhere in the greenery. The little cove was more sheltered from the wind than other parts she'd encountered on her walk. She was surprised to find she felt so relaxed in this spot, at this time of year, but mused that most people enjoyed being on the edge of the sea. Perhaps it was because, lost in the history of time, humans had come from the sea and still felt a constant, ancient pull to be close to it whenever they could.

She was roused from her reverie with a start as a shadow fell across her.

'Good afternoon! May I ask what you are doing here, and how you got on to Coomer?'

2

Jill jumped at the sound of a human voice. She opened her eyes and squinted up at a youngish man with dark hair, strong features and an evenly tanned skin. She unfolded her legs and stood up. He was a lot taller than she was, and a lot broader. He was well groomed and dressed in no-nonsense corduroys, green wellingtons and a Barbour jacket, but none of that was any guarantee that he wasn't a serial killer.

She cleared her throat nervously. 'Good afternoon. I'm Jill Douglas, and you are . . . ?'

He thrust his large hands into his pockets, viewing her suspiciously. His voice was composed. 'My name is Blake Armand. I'm the warden of this island. You're trespassing!' His eyes were expressionless as he waited for her reaction.

Jill smiled weakly, torn between relief that he was a perfectly normal human being, and slight annoyance because he clearly disapproved of her presence. Schooled in remaining polite in all situations, she held out her hand to him. 'I'm pleased to meet you, Mr Armand. My firm has been commissioned to sell Coomer and I came here to see it for myself. Photos are never as good as reality, are they?'

Reluctantly he reached out and shook her hand briefly. The expression on his face hardened. 'I knew that the family were thinking of selling, but I wasn't aware that things were already on the move. I had hoped to persuade them to extend the lease to the conservation board.'

Jill met his cold eyes and tried to sound friendly. 'You can't really blame the family if they've decided to sell, can you? If they never come here, and have no intention of visiting it in the future, they may as well.'

Blake's voice was coloured by slightly

sarcastic tones. 'Yes, I suppose so — if pounds and pence are the only things that matter. It just happens that it's now the home of a large number of birds, some small mammals and seals, and fish also flourish around the shores. If the Trust had more time, we might find a way to keep it as it is — an unspoiled biotope.'

Jill coloured slightly. 'Well, perhaps you'll be lucky and no one will be interested; in that case, the family may agree to extend the trust's lease.' She added cheerily, 'Perhaps you might even persuade your employers to buy it themselves?'

'So that you'll get your commission? As long as someone buys it, you couldn't care less, could you?'

She stiffened, and gave up trying to be pleasant. 'Finding buyers is my job. I'm not employed to think about the principles or ethics behind a sale. Everyone has a reason for selling their property; sometimes it's a good one, sometimes bad — but it's absolutely none of my business.' Tossing her head, she went on, 'And just for your information, I do not see Coomer merely in terms of pounds and pence — I'm pleasantly surprised. I can understand why you would like to retain it in its present state, but you ought to have this argument with the owners — not me!' There were bright spots of colour on her cheeks.

He ran a hand over his face and viewed her speculatively again. 'No, you're right. I shouldn't bicker with you.' He tried to normalise the atmosphere again. 'How did you get here?'

She steadied her thoughts and followed his lead. 'Jack Lewis brought me here, and he told me I can walk back at low tide — ' She looked at her watch. 'In thirty minutes or so.'

His glance slid over her, from top to toe. 'Well, at least someone told you how to dress.' He looked at his watch. 'Have you seen everything? There aren't many birds here at the moment, but once nesting time starts the whole place is buzzing with activity. They've got used to the fact that the island is uninhabited, and so it's a perfect breeding ground for them.'

Jill nodded. 'I've seen as much as I can. It's pretty wild and overgrown but very attractive. I wish I could have seen the inside of the house, but it's locked. I'll have to find out about a key.'

Briskly he answered, 'No need for that. Follow me!' He turned on his heel and started back up the slope towards the house.

Jill scrambled after him, glad he didn't notice it was an effort for her to keep pace with him. Clearly, he was very fit. He strode upwards as if he was strolling along the beach in St Tropez. Jill mused that he'd probably make a very good figure on a beach, wherever he was.

He reached the porch ahead of her. Bending, he lifted a large stone alongside the wall and held a key aloft, before inserting it in the lock and opening the door. He made a sweeping gesture and stood aside. There was a hint of amusement in his eyes as she passed him and went in.

The place smelled musty, and disuse was evident everywhere. An old-fashioned hall stand housed some walking sticks and umbrellas. The stone-flagged floor was covered in dust, and a couple of gloomy oil paintings hung on the walls. One door led off into the kitchen, one to the dining room and a third to the sitting room.

Jill didn't waste much time looking at them; she knew what they were like from her external inspections. She turned her attention to the stairs. The broad handrail was plain and solid in design. There were three bedrooms; two small, and the larger main bedroom. They were furnished with outdated, conventional furniture. The beds were covered in yellowed dustsheets. The bathroom looked as if it had never been fashionable and there were thick brown rings in the washbasin, toilet and bathtub. Jill wondered if the island had its own water supply, and if it was connected to the electricity supply.

She skipped downstairs again, went outside and found Blake Armand lounging against a tree. She wouldn't have been surprised if he'd left her to her fate — but perhaps he just wanted to make sure she locked the door and was off his terrain.

Jill locked the door, replaced the key under the stone, and then turned to face him. 'Thanks! Nothing sensational but it's a solid little house, and it's still basically in good condition. Is there a water and electricity supply?'

He straightened up and stuck his hands into his pockets. 'There's fresh water from a well, and the house is connected to the electricity supply. At present, the electricity is disconnected — with no one living here, it would be a waste of money. Unless I'm wrong, the house needs rewiring — the present electrical system is probably life-threatening.'

'A *well*?' Jill repeated. 'Do you mean you have to collect water in a bucket, like Snow White?'

One corner of his mouth turned up. 'Yes, but when the electricity is connected, Snow White can let a pump do the work for her.'

'And it's safe to drink? Where's the well?'

'Round the side; over there.' He nodded in the right direction. 'It's perfectly safe — I often make myself a hot drink when I spend any time here.' He noticed her puzzled expression, and before she could ask how, he answered. 'I brought over a gas-burner with cartridges and some tea and coffee — they're in the kitchen.' He looked at his watch. 'I'm leaving now, and it's almost time for you to leave, too. Do you want a lift back to Jack's, or do you prefer to walk?'

Jill reflected on the two possibilities quickly, and decided to accept his offer. He wasn't a particularly amiable character, but the sky was full of threatening grey clouds and rain wasn't far off. The wind was on the increase, too. A quick trip with him was more tempting than a solitary walk in the rain. 'If it's no trouble, I'll come with you.'

He nodded and began to walk in the direction of the jetty. She dogged his footsteps. He made no attempt to make conversation, and neither did she.

A small boat was bobbing on the water next to the jetty. He got in and she scrambled awkwardly after him, sitting down on the narrow plank-like bench and holding onto the side as he revved the motor and untied the craft.

They moved out into the flow and let the slow-moving current speed them on their way. It was a matter of minutes before Jill spotted Jack Lewis' boat tied to a ring set into a rock on the bank. It was making tinny sounds as it hit the pebbles along the bank. Blake throttled the engine and drew in to the side. Jill hoped she wouldn't land ignominiously on her bottom when she sprang, but the manoeuvre went smoothly and her well-ingtons cushioned her landing beautifully.

'Thanks, Mr Armand!'

He nodded silently. His dark eyes seemed to linger on her for a few seconds before he guided the boat out into the channel again without further delay.

Jill ambled along to the makeshift steps leading up to the roadway, and watched his boat disappear from sight.

What a disagreeable man! As she staggered up the steep steps, she told herself that he probably spent so much time with wildlife that he considered human beings beneath his attention. Generally, people liked her, and she didn't often need to convince them that she was a gentle soul without a bone of nastiness in her.

She threw back her shoulders, reached the verge and headed across to Jack's house. After announcing her return to his wife, she thanked them again and then drove back to the pub. In some ways, she was glad to be going back tomorrow to the office and her slightly cockeyed boss; at least she felt comfortable with him, and she knew he liked and appreciated her.

★   ★   ★

Crunching along a frosty path, Jill felt cheery; what could be more wonderful for anyone than being at home for Christmas?

Her parents lived in an old farm-house; the hills rose on either side of it and the house nestled in a grove of trees that had been planted long ago to provide maximum shelter from the wind. To their delight, one of Jill's brothers had finally decided he wanted to manage the farm, and now things were in a transition stage.

Jill only hoped her parents could let go, and step back, otherwise conflict between them and her brother and his wife would be inevitable. Her brother had new ideas and other plans for the future; he didn't want to remain simply a sheep farmer, he wanted to branch out in other directions.

Bundled up against the cold, she and her father were making their way to collect holly from a tree in the nearby coppice. She looked up at the sky briefly, as they walked along a pathway between the hedges and drystone walls. The weak winter sun had disappeared a long time ago and the air was fresh and cold. She felt childish delight when she noticed snow had begun to fall. Small, light snowflakes were drifting down like thistledown through the still air. She took a deep, exhilarating breath and thrust her hands deeper into her pockets.

'Snow! A white Christmas! I couldn't have arranged it better!'

Mr Douglas laughed. 'Don't be so conceited! Only God can arrange that. But I admit snow at Christmas is perfect, isn't it?' He was big-framed, with a thin face and bushy eyebrows. His eyes were closely set and their sparkle showed no sign of his age.

'Good thing Gary and I brought the sheep down from the higher ground a couple of weeks ago,' he commented.

Jill took her cue. 'You don't mind — passing on the control of everything to Gary? It'll be hard for you trying not to interfere with his ideas and plans — you realise that, don't you?'

He stopped and turned to her, the start of a grin on his face. 'I know that, love. I promise I won't interfere. I can still remember what it was like when I took over from my dad. He meddled and made my life hell for years. Everyone has to make their own mistakes and gain their own experiences.

'Your mum and I have talked things through. You might not believe it, but we're looking forward to taking a back seat and having more time for joining in with village life a bit more. Your mother has made up her mind we're going to learn to dance — would you believe it, at our age! There's a course starting at the village hall in a couple of week's time.'

'Really? What a wonderful idea! Tuxedos and tulle — *Strictly Come Dancing*, here we come, eh!'

He laughed and they walked on. 'How are things with you?'

'Me? Fine. Not very much on our books at the moment — but it often slows down before Christmas. That's why I got a few extra days' holiday and why John decided to close the office down until the New Year. The real reason is that he wanted to fly to Morocco with some friends this week, but he wouldn't tell us that, of course. And Clive and I didn't spoil his fun and give any sign we'd twigged on to him!'

'Funny chap, that John. I know you like him, but I don't think I could put up working with him for long. Too namby-pamby for my taste.'

'Oh, he's all right. Lots of people seem to think he's spineless — they're misled by the way he acts. It's deceptive; underneath the boyish façade he's a tough cookie and a sharp businessman. He also sticks up for his friends and people he likes. He grumbles and carps at me and Clive about our work all the time, but if an outsider says a single wrong word about us, he springs at their throat like a Doberman in a rage!'

They'd reached their destination and Jill clambered up onto the drystone wall. She considered where best to cut the branches of shiny bottle-green spiky leaves with scarlet berries. It would be self-punishing to take too much from the same place every year and leave big holes. Reaching out with a pair of secateurs, she began to snip away.

'Aren't we lucky to have our own holly tree? I just can't imagine Christmas without doing this with you every year.'

Her father picked up the bounty she threw to him and stuffed it into a hemp sack. 'So, what about a boyfriend? You do realise that your mother is dying to organise your wedding, don't you?'

'Have to disappoint her there, I'm afraid. I try to ignore all her hints about how welcome I am to bring a friend home with me, but you must admit it was a catastrophe the last time I tried. She tells Darren the same thing about bringing a girlfriend year after year — but he hasn't taken any notice, either!'

Her father nodded sympathetically. 'That chap you brought last year didn't fit in with us at all. I didn't say anything at the time, of course, but I honestly didn't think you were suited.'

Stuffing her escaping scarf back deeper into her collar, Jill agreed. 'The closest Brian had ever been to the country before last Christmas was the vegetables in the supermarket. He couldn't gel with my interest in the sheep or the farm, and you know how much I love being here — despite the draughts, the cold winds, and the sense of isolation. If nothing else, it made me realise how different our attitudes were.'

She shrugged and clipped another twig. 'I see him now and then, we're still friends, but I know very well we wouldn't survive as a pair much beyond the wedding reception. It would be great to fall in love with someone everybody likes.'

'That's not what matters, and you know it. I didn't particularly like your grandfather, or he me, but we got along because we both wanted your mother to be happy. Find someone you can love and respect; then the rest will fall into place.' He asked, more tentatively, 'So is there someone on the horizon, then?'

Jill laughed and shook her head. 'No — I'd like to stay married to the same man all my life; second-best won't do for me, and that's a hard nut to crack these days. Actually I'm not worried if I never do find the perfect companion — luckily we women are independent and self-sufficient these days. You don't have to be married to have a good life.'

'Huh! Tell that to your mother and see how she reacts.'

Jill grinned. 'I know. Have we got enough?'

'I think so. Come on.' He reached out his hand. 'Let's go back and have some coffee laced with something to warm us up again.'

Jill took his roughened, work-weathered hand and jumped down.

'What a wonderful idea! I must admit I'm getting soft, living in town. I need some toughening up — I never used to feel the cold, or mind traipsing around with the wind freezing my bones, but nowadays the attractions of central heating and an easy life are encouraging me to be a couch potato!'

★　★　★

Jill swivelled to and fro in her office chair and gazed out of the window. Christmas had been a delight, and she was grateful to have such a warm and wonderful family. She got on well with her sister-in-law, loved her two brothers to bits, and her parents were just perfect. Apart from a couple of teenage years when she had felt the need to be mutinous, she and her parents had always been close.

She noticed John, well-tanned from his Moroccan sojourn, was on his way across to her desk with some papers in his hand. She turned her attention to straightening her knee-length soft wool skirt and pale green turtle-neck jumper, and then to sorting a pile of papers that lay on her desk. By the time John reached her side, she looked immaculate — and she also looked very busy.

Waving the papers at her with one hand, John straightened his silk tie, in shades of mauve and green, with the other. 'My pet, the advertisements we put in the London papers over Christmas have paid off. Just guess who's just been on the phone about your little island?'

'I can't imagine.'

'Try! Who would have enough money to spare for an island?'

Getting slightly impatient, Jill replied, 'John, is this a quiz, twenty questions, or what? Are you going to tell me, or not?'

Triumphantly, he announced, 'Clyde Chapman!'

From John's expression, Jill realised he must be well-known. She didn't want to show her ignorance, but she had no other choice.

'And, er, who is Clyde Chapman?'

His eyes widened. 'You have *never heard* of Clyde Chapman? Do you live with the rest of us on this planet? He's the lead singer with The Ghosts.'

'Really? Who are The Ghosts?'

'Jill, you evidently have a giant gap in your knowledge bank. The Ghosts are a world-famous rock band. I would have thought someone of your age would light up like a neon sign at the mere mention of their name.'

'They clearly aren't my cup of tea, otherwise I'd know the name, wouldn't I? Anyway — what does it matter whether I'm mad about their musical genius or not? The main thing is that they may be prospective customers for Coomer Island!'

'True. However, the whole band is

not interested — just the frontman, Clyde Chapman — and for Heaven's sake, don't you make the mistake of not appearing knowledgeable about his background. These people are usually narcissistic; I have a friend who is a concert pianist, and if I say one wrong word about his playing skills, he sulks for weeks after — so be warned!'

He handed her a paper. 'Here's the telephone number and address of his manager. You'll have to get in touch with him and find out when Clyde can come to take a look round. As far as I understand, the group is on tour at present, but they are having a break fairly soon. You're not likely to find anyone else before then, but you'll need to keep in touch with this chap, and keep the kettle on the boil. Pretend others are interested; that sort of thing.'

'John, I have no intention of lying to anyone, for any reason.'

'My dear, there is no necessity to be untruthful — just drop a few indirect hints, mislead them a little to think there may be some other interested prospective buyers!'

Jill looked at the paper. 'You never stop trying, do you?'

'In any case, you wouldn't be lying — there really is some competition. Some chap from a nearby wildlife countryside park has been in touch about the island too.'

Jill looked up quickly as the image of Blake Armand came to mind. 'Oh? Who was that?'

'Can't remember the name. He was a warden, nice deep voice, and he sounded like a pleasant chap. He wanted the address of the owners, and from what I gathered, he was intending to try to persuade them to reduce the price and sell the island to the nature reserve. I gave him the number, because I don't think he'll have much luck with them. They are after big money, as much as we can harvest for them. He's sending me some gen about the nature reserve just for our information; I expect he's hoping that we'll all read it, feel thoroughly sympathetic, and jump on his bandwagon if we get the chance.'

Jill contacted Clyde Chapman's manager and found out it would be several weeks before she could arrange a viewing.

Reporting back on the situation to John, she asked casually, 'Do you know why he is interested?'

'I expect he's accumulated too much money too fast! All stars want to own a mansion in Surrey, a castle in Scotland, a cottage in Herefordshire, a Caribbean island, or the like. Clyde was born not far from Coomer and he probably has a thing about owning something sizeable in the district. Mad, if you ask me; he won't even have time to enjoy it, if his success continues.'

'But it makes it more understandable. I'll be in touch with his manager in a couple of weeks, just before the tour ends. I'll fit in a viewing for him whenever he has time.'

She paused. 'Needless to say, there's no guarantee that someone else won't grab it before then, but to be honest, at the moment there is no serious rival in sight.'

★   ★   ★

The back of the winter was broken. The days were growing longer, and the temperatures were climbing gradually again. Jill noticed there were the first signs of buds on the trees and bushes, and the first crocuses and snowdrops were already parading their colours and improving people's moods. She'd sold several houses in the intervening weeks, and she took great pleasure in finding people just what they wanted.

Sometimes she almost felt like Cinderella's fairy godmother when she succeeded in connecting the right person to exactly the right house.

Blake Armand did send John some brochures, which he passed on to Jill. She flipped through them, reading about the nature reserve and the surrounding district. He'd also included some leaflets about points of interest and things to do. She spotted him pictured on one of the nature reserve leaflets amidst a group of people surveying an impressive view of the countryside far below. It wasn't a wonderful photo of him, but Jill recognised his tall figure and good features straight away. He was smiling at the group surrounding him, and she thought how well the smile suited him. She'd experienced him as a dour and grim person but, evidently, he had more than one side to his character.

She picked up a leaflet about an activity weekend at a nearby outdoor centre — one day walking, and another day rock-climbing and canoeing. She remembered her conversation with her father about growing soft. A weekend like that would be just the thing to toughen her up a bit. According to the leaflet, the course was organised and run by a woman. It certainly didn't sound as if the nearby nature reserve had anything directly to do with it, so Jill decided to phone and find out.

The phone rang several times and the

woman who finally answered sounded a little out of breath. 'Good morning. Ascent Training, Sharon Burton speaking, can I help you?'

'Morning. I'd like to make enquiries about a weekend course I found in your leaflet — about walking, rock-climbing and canoeing.'

'When are you thinking of coming?'

'Beginning of March?'

'That's no trouble. What do you want to know?'

'Do I need experience, who does the tuition, and where can I stay?'

'No experience necessary. The courses are intended to introduce people to the various sports. I'm in charge, but there is another instructor who helps out with the rock-climbing and canoeing, and whoever is available takes charge of the walking.'

That sounded quite straightforward to Jill — there was no mention of a warden or ranger or such. 'And accommodation?'

'We have unpretentious but good accommodation, separate male and female double rooms. It depends how many people take part, whether you'll have to share a room or not.'

'Are meals inclusive?'

'Yes, someone from the nearby village comes in to cook for us. If you arrive on Friday evening, which is advisable, you are entitled to two evening meals and two breakfasts. We also supply soup and sandwiches for lunch breaks during the day.'

'It sounds good but I'm not terribly fit, and I'm scared of heights.'

'We don't aim to get you trained for the Olympics! As long as you are healthy and prepared to make an effort, that's fine. We only train on small rocks to start with; you'll have to see how you cope. If you feel you can't manage, just say so. Oh — the only other thing is, we don't stop for bad weather. So unless there's a hurricane in the offing, the course goes on, rain or no rain.'

Jill felt reassured. It was something to look forward to; new activities. She'd never tried canoeing or rock climbing.

'Right. I'll just read it all through again, and then if I'm still interested, I'll send you an email booking. Will that be okay?'

'Fine! As soon as we've booked you in, you get a confirmation and then you have to make your deposit within ten days!'

After consideration, Jill decided she would go. It sounded interesting and a bit of a challenge.

3

After only a few calls, Jill managed to fix a viewing appointment with Clyde Chapman and his manager.

A week before the date, she packed her bag with the right kind of clothing and set off straight from work at the end of the day. She had no difficulty in finding the activity centre; she got there just before the last glimmer of dusk was fading. The centre was off the same main road that passed the pub where she'd stayed a couple of months ago; it was further along in the opposite direction, but easy to find.

She parked her Mini neatly next to some other cars and got out to look around. There was a handful of converted old cottages clustered around a sleek modern building standing askew in the middle. The modern structure was the office; she knocked and went in.

A young woman looked up. She was small and dark, with round brown eyes. She viewed Jill sceptically, taking in Jill's smart suit and medium heels. Jill could tell Sharon Burton was probably thinking that she was unsuited to take part in any kind of activity course.

She closed the door. 'Hi, I'm Jill Douglas.'

The other woman nodded. 'Hi! You found us without any trouble?'

Jill nodded. 'No trouble. The way here is well sign-posted.'

'I'm Sharon. I'll mark you in as arrived and then show you where you're staying. There are five of you on this weekend's course altogether — three men and two women — so you and the other girl can each have a room to yourself.' She flipped open a ledger, ran her finger down the list, and marked something off with a large tick. She closed it with a thud and came round the desk with a key in her hand. 'Follow me! The evening meal will be in two hours' time. I hope the others will have

50

arrived by then. Come across for a drink when you've unpacked — the main eating and meeting room is just over there, in the converted cottage with the green door. We start tomorrow morning with canoeing. Have you done any canoeing?'

Jill strolled at her side; she was a little taller than the other woman. 'No, but I've always wanted to find out what it was like.'

'Well, this is a perfect chance to do that.'

They reached one of the cottages and Sharon went on ahead. She gestured to the downstairs rooms from the narrow hallway. 'To the left, the sitting room, to the right, the kitchen. Upstairs are two bedrooms and the bathroom is in between. You can take your pick, as you are the first arrival. The other girl will be sleeping in the other room. There's a lock on the bedroom door, of course. Make yourself comfortable, and I'll see you later.' She placed the door key on the hallway table.

'Thanks! That's great.'

Sharon gave her a somewhat restrained, polite smile, turned and left.

The bedroom Jill chose was Spartan in appearance, but clean. The window looked out on to the windswept hill behind the centre. Even though spring was starting to show in most places, here the grass still looked dry and untamed.

She unpacked, changed into jeans, a thick hooded sweatshirt, and an ultra-light nylon jacket. A walk down to the pebbled beach was just what she needed after a day in the office.

★   ★   ★

Jill had slept like a log. Breakfast was at eight. Jill could tell Sharon Burton was relieved to see that she was wearing suitable clothing. The other participants seemed a friendly, mixed bunch, and although they were all cautious for a few minutes, one of them — an outgoing young chap — soon had them all chatting and getting to know one another better.

'So, when you've finished breakfast, we'll be leaving to go to a local river. It is one of the shallowest around here, so if you do fall in, apart from getting soaked, nothing much will happen. You must wear a life-jacket all the time, no matter what, and a helmet. We'll just give you the basic instructions on how to paddle and control a canoe. Each of you has your own canoe.

'If you become real enthusiasts, you will need to learn other things like how to roll the canoe, for example — that's usually done in an indoor pool until you are absolutely sure of your ability to cope. We are only showing you the basics this morning. This is Danny — he's my fellow instructor — so if you want to know anything, you can ask either of us.'

Danny was a pleasant-faced, athletic thirty-year-old with blond straggly hair that stood out like a dandelion fringe around his head, and friendly blue eyes.

He lifted his hand to them all in greeting.

They all packed into the company van with canoes loaded behind them on a trailer. After a short journey, they found themselves on an open section of hard banking next to a slow-flowing river. They had to practise a sweeping stroke on dry land, were told about how incorrect paddling would send them in the wrong direction, and useful advice such as the canoe having a natural desire to turn to the right if you were paddling on the left.

Suitably dressed and informed, they helped unload the canoes, and one by one they took to the water like cautious ducks. Jill enjoyed it. She had no doubt that her arms would complain grievously tomorrow, but she tried her best to absorb any advice she got from either Sharon or Danny. They were flitting back and forth between all the participants, like busy dragonflies on the water.

Danny gave her a wicked grin and

winked whenever Jill succeeded in doing what he told her to. She decided canoeing was fun. Tiring — but fun. They succeeded in travelling along a section of the river, and manoeuvring around to paddle in the other direction back to the starting point. Time passed quickly.

Jill was sorry when she heard Danny shouting from the bank. 'That's it! Time to re-load the canoes and return to the centre.'

Amid their protests, he continued. 'Rock climbing is scheduled for this afternoon. Save your energies! When we get back, you'll only have a short break for some soup, sandwiches and a hot drink and then it'll soon be time for everyone to meet up down on the beach again.'

Thankfully, Danny was around to help load the canoes. He'd done it so often it was second nature to him, although most of them had difficulty. The canoes weren't heavy in comparison to their size — but they were awkward to handle for a novice. Another male participant and Jill helped each other lifting their canoes, and Danny positioned them correctly on the trailer.

Jill turned to the instructor. 'Thanks, Danny. I've really enjoyed myself this morning. It won't be the last time I try canoeing!'

He nodded, satisfied. 'Good! Then we've done what we hope to achieve — sparked some interest!'

Jill was taking off her life-jacket when a tall, shadowy figure strode out of the trees nearby. Her heart skipped a beat when she realised it was Blake Armand. How silly — why would it do that? Her colour mounted and she pretended to be occupied with her helmet straps.

Sharon rushed over to him. 'Blake — I haven't seen you all week. I've missed you.'

Jill had a feeling that if Sharon Burton had been a spouting fountain, at that moment the bowl would be overflowing the brim.

Blake viewed Sharon with vague interest, but his expression was bland. 'Really? Why? Have I forgotten something?'

His voice carried clearly across the open space and Jill couldn't help noticing how Sharon placed her hand possessively on his lower arm. Although Jill tried to take no notice, his deep voice made her extremely aware of his presence.

Sharon was reassuring him. 'No, of course not.'

'Good. I just wondered if I'd overlooked a vital meeting or some such thing.' His eyes skimmed the group, pausing when he spotted Jill, but he gave no immediate sign that he recognised her.

'You are too competent and too proficient to forget anything important,' Sharon flattered the ranger shamelessly.

Jill smiled to herself at the thought of how her younger colleague Clive would have reacted to Jill's sickly sweet behaviour. It seemed that with little encouragement from Blake Armand,

Sharon Burton was grovelling; she must be totally besotted with him. Jill couldn't tell from where she was standing whether he appreciated the interest or not.

Jill turned her back on the two of them, uncertain as she did so why she didn't want to face him. She felt something touching her hand; it was soft and warm. A black shaggy dog of indeterminate origins was licking her hand. She automatically began to stroke its head, and crouched down to look into its trusting brown eyes. 'Hello! Who are you?'

Without looking up, she sensed Blake had come across. 'His name is Laurence. He's my dog. What are you doing here?'

His stare was bold and travelled over her face. As at their last meeting on Coomer Island, Jill had gained the impression that he was someone who generally liked to have everything under control.

There was a slight tingling in the pit of her stomach as she stood up. 'Hello,

Mr Armand. I'm on a weekend course at the activity centre. I knew the nature reserve is near here, but I didn't expect to see you.'

Sharon hurried across to join them and looked from the one to the other with traces of suspicion on her face. 'Do you know each other?'

Blake Armand kept his eyes on Jill's face. 'Yes, we've met before.'

'Oh!' Sharon sounded put out.

Out of the corner of her eye, Jill noticed that Danny and the others had finished loading the canoes; she was glad of a genuine excuse to move away. She met his glance and gave him a courteous smile. 'It was nice to meet you again.' She didn't expect a reaction and didn't get one. She bent down and stroked the dog again, tickling him behind the ears.

'Bye, Laurence! Good boy.' The dog waved his tail in appreciation.

Jill turned away and joined the others getting into the van. She was almost relieved that there hadn't been time to

59

make any more polite conversation. She liked his dog more than she liked him — no, that wasn't true. Yet she couldn't define why she felt uneasy about Blake Armand. Perhaps he was married with a couple of children, or paired up with Sharon, or with someone else. He was an attractive man. Those steel-grey eyes were magnetic and his personality afforded him a special, indefinable kind of aura.

The other course participants were talking noisily to each other in the back of the van. Jill took the seat next to Danny and decided to ask a few questions. There was no harm in that.

'Are Sharon and Blake Armand a couple? They seem very close.'

Danny grinned. 'No, I don't think so. Sharon wouldn't mind, I'm sure, but he's resisted so far. You know him?'

Jill looked out at the passing scenery. 'Not very well. I've met him before — through my job. I was just wondering, that's all.'

'Blake's okay. He's a straightforward

character; no messing about — you know where you stand with him. He helped Sharon and me avoid a couple of fiascos when we first opened the centre. There's a lot of red tape involved in running this sort of thing, and he knows his way around.

'He's a decent chap. He's reserved, but he gets things done and he's well-liked locally.'

Jill nodded. She wondered why Blake Armand was occupying her thoughts so much. She searched around for another topic of conversation, and before long she had Danny telling her all about the ups and downs he'd experienced while helping to run the centre.

★   ★   ★

The weekend group was gathered around a huge boulder near the beach. Jill had succeeded in pushing Blake Armand from her mind and was concentrating on what Danny was teaching them about knots and safety precautions. They'd already done some adequate warm-up exercises and stretching. Each of them was wearing a harness.

When he was satisfied they understood how important safety and his instructions were, Danny demonstrated how he found niches for his hands and feet. He proceeded to attach protection as he made his way gradually up the rock face until he reached the top.

It was large, but not impossibly high, so Jill had no qualms about trying when her time came. Sharon Burton was steadying the rope from below, and Danny from above. It was a lot more difficult than it looked. Even though she'd borrowed the right kind of climbing shoes from a friend, finding support for her feet and a safe grip for her hands was easier said than done. She lost her hold once, but the guiding ropes were taut enough to cope with the result and a few seconds later she swung back against the face of the rock, and could continue on her way.

At the top, Danny clapped. 'Well

done! You made it!'

Jill felt jubilant. 'My fingers feel as if they're about to drop off, and I would definitely have fallen if you two hadn't secured my climb, but otherwise I really enjoyed it.'

'Good! Now you must abseil down. The rope is always there and you can't fall. Go backwards off the rock in your own time, and when you get to the bottom you can watch the others and decide if you want to do it again!'

It was daunting, especially the first thrust backwards, but once she felt confident that her descent was being controlled and bolstered from above and below, Jill forgot about what could go wrong, and found herself back on firm ground much faster than she had expected.

Jill felt pleased with her first attempt at climbing. She was full of interest as she watched the remaining participants have a go. Some were faster and more confident than others, but soon all five of them completed their climb. Sharon called them together.

'We have plenty of time left, and you've all managed climbing the boulder well, so I think we can move on a step further and attempt climbing a fissure now — a kind of funnel in the rock that narrows slightly towards the top. It's more difficult than what you just did, but the principles of climbing are the same. I'm sure it will boost your egos if you manage it.'

The other four nodded and looked satisfied as they set off to go further down the beach. Reluctantly, Jill followed them. She knew her own limits and her own fears, but she didn't want to make a fool of herself and admit she was scared so she went along anyway.

The rock in question was standing alone, not as high as the nearby cliffs, but in Jill's eyes, it was immense. It stretched up over seventy feet into the air and sea water had split it in the centre, creating a funnel-shaped crevice. Jill stepped back automatically as she contemplated it. Her pulse increased and she began to feel uncomfortable.

Danny took the lead and established protection aids as he climbed. Once he'd reached the peak and taken up position to handle the ropes, one of the other course members who'd done particularly well on the boulder climb began his ascent. Danny knew the fissure like the back of his hand, and the course member looked uncertain and inept in comparison, but he got there in the end and abseiled down to the encouraging applause of the others waiting below. Jill watched the happenings in silence.

Then Sharon called out, 'Come on, Jill!'

Her heart pounding, she answered, 'I'd rather not. I have this thing about heights — I don't think I can manage.'

'Nonsense! You managed the first boulder perfectly well; this really isn't as bad as you're imagining it is. You'll hardly notice the height at all because of the funnel shape. Have a go. Danny and I will back you up all the way!'

'B-but . . . ' Jill stammered.

'No buts. We never ask anyone to do anything that is beyond their abilities. This is within yours. Don't chicken out. You're being silly!' Sharon came across and briskly attached the clips to Jill's safety harness. 'Come on, don't think — just climb, like you did before!'

Jill felt a growing sense of unreality as Sharon took her by her shoulders and propelled her to the base of the fissure. It was dark and damp on the sandy bottom, and a quick look up reassured her a little when she saw Danny looking down at her. She tried to steady her nerves and remember how she'd managed the first rock. She started to climb, and for a while, she thought she'd manage it after all, but then she made a fatal error and looked down. Her heartbeat accelerated out of control, her breath shortened, and she began to feel extremely sick. She was glued to the face of the rock and couldn't imagine how she'd ever be able to move forward or back. She felt she would never be able to move anywhere ever again.

'Keep going!' Sharon's voice echoed against the rock surface.

Jill couldn't have kept going even if someone had tried to force her to with a machine gun. Sheer gut-wrenching panic engulfed her and she clung on desperately.

'Jill, keep going! Climb! Climb! Don't be a goose, you can do it!'

Jill's throat was dry; her voice was strained, frightened and barely audible. 'I can't! I can't! I'm sorry. I'm too scared out of my wits to do anything!'

'Don't be *stupid*. Take a deep breath and go on!'

Jill wished she could die. Down below, she heard the rest of the group talking excitedly, continual sounds, movements and clatter.

Suddenly there was a new voice among the others. Blake Armand's.

'Jill — I'm coming. I'm going to bring you down; hang on.'

Jill was positive she couldn't have

done anything else even if she tried; she closed her eyes, waited and listened as she heard him climbing. He came closer and closer, but she couldn't look down to see where he was — she would have been sick all over him.

All of a sudden, he was straddling the rock and positioned behind her. He put an arm round her waist. 'I've got you, and I'm going to fix an extra rope. Then you'll have to cling on to me and we'll go down together. Just look at me, or straight ahead — don't attempt to look anywhere else! Just trust me; do you think you can do that?'

With tears pricking at the back of her eyes, she nodded. She was glad he couldn't see her face. 'Yes, I think so. What are you doing here anyway? This isn't part of your job.'

Deftly securing the ropes while talking to her, he said casually, 'Oh, I just wanted to see how you were getting on.'

She didn't think to ask him why he had been so interested. 'Not very well, as you can tell!' She attempted to inject some lightness into her voice.

'Don't worry about that. Sharon should never have let you try. You're scared of heights, aren't you?'

She nodded ashamedly.

'Why didn't you just tell her so?'

'I did, but perhaps she didn't realise just how scared I am.'

'My sister has the same problem.'

'Oh!' Jill gasped. He'd finished knotting them together and had turned her towards him. Gripping her tightly and with no space between them, he murmured, 'Ready?'

She could feel his warm breath on her face as she stared into his dark eyes. She did trust him; he was someone you could trust, she was sure of that. 'Yes, I think so.'

Right, I'll push off and you just cling on. If it helps, close your eyes and leave the rest to me.'

Jill decided that was a very good idea and did so. She felt, with the heightened awareness that came with adrenalin, the firmness of his body, the swinging motion as they descended, and the occasional collision of the rock wall and his shoes. Sooner than she expected, she could open her eyes again — they were back on the firm sand, and people gathered around them to loosen the knots and free them.

Jill flushed with embarrassment. Everyone was sympathetic, but she felt like a stupid fool. At the earliest moment possible she tried to escape.

'Excuse me!' she stuttered. 'Thanks, everyone. I'll go back to the centre. Please don't bother any more. I'm all right now, honestly!'

Sharon looked repentant, but Jill wondered cynically whether that was because she sympathised — or because Blake had witnessed her misjudgment of the situation.

Jill picked up her rucksack from the sand and almost stumbled in her attempt to get away from the others as fast as she could. She'd only gone a few yards before Blake caught up and grabbed her arm.

'Jill — there's no reason for you to feel bad. Anyone can be scared of heights, and it can happen at any time, and any age. Usually the cause is deep-seated, and something special triggers it off.'

He turned her gently to face him and showed no surprise at the tears running down her face. He pulled her into his arms and simply held her.

She felt stupid and foolish, but his embrace helped subdue the effects of her distress, and she felt secure in his arms. There was a sandalwood scent about him, and he was solid and substantial. She let her resistance fade and remained in his arms until she felt strong enough to step back.

Brushing the tears away with the back of her hand, she tried a tremulous smile. 'Thanks! I feel such a fool. I can't stop myself feeling scared. I've tried to get over it on various occasions, but nothing helps. I should have refused to climb outright. Don't blame Sharon; it was my fault for not being more resolute and just refusing to do it. The first rock was okay, because it really was fairly small, but that other one was way beyond my capability.'

With a shaky voice, she attempted to sound more laid-back. 'I find that I can manage to do the climbing bit, but I get collywobbles if I look where I've come from and where I'm going.'

He studied her for a few seconds. The sea breezes were playing havoc with his dark hair. 'Don't make excuses for Sharon. She is responsible for everyone on the course; that's part of her job. If she knew you were scared of heights beforehand, you should never have been forced to do any climbing unless you wanted to. From what I understand, she pushed you into this situation.' The muscles in his jaw were clenched. He ran his hand through his hair. 'Why don't you have a hot bath? It'll loosen your muscles and help you to relax. Once you've had a hot meal, the world will look a lot brighter again, promise.' He gave her an encouraging smile.

The smile helped more than the words and Jill gave him a grateful look. He reached forward and stroked away the remains of some tears on her cheek with his thumb. She almost flinched at his touch but managed to suppress the reaction, which took her by surprise.

'Yes, that's a very good idea. Thank you, Mr Armand! You saved my life in more ways than one today.'

He snorted. 'For Heaven's sake, woman, will you just call me Blake — you make me feel like Methuselah when you keep calling me Mister all the time!'

She gave a shaky laugh. 'All right — I will, and I'm Jill.'

He thrust his hands into his pocket. 'I already know that.'

Jill suddenly realised he hadn't even been properly equipped to climb. He was wearing trekking boots, ordinary trousers and a short corduroy jacket. He must be a good climber to have coped so well. Why had he taken over, and not Sharon or Danny? She was reluctant to ask, so she just nodded and headed towards the buildings.

She didn't look back. If she had done, she'd have seen that Blake Armand was standing and watching her progress for much longer than was strictly necessary.

4

A hot bath certainly did help, Jill found. The steaming, rose-scented water loosened her muscles and made her comfortably drowsy.

Sharon came across to see her as daylight was fading. Her face suffused with heightened colour, she made her apologies. 'I really didn't believe you were so scared. It's been a lesson for me. In future, I'll make sure that no one who shows any reluctance will face a dangerous situation like that again because of my stupidity. I'm sorry!'

Jill waved her hand. 'Don't worry. It was as much my fault as yours for not categorically refusing in the first case. I feel such a fool!'

'Don't. Everyone sympathises. Come across with me now. The evening meal is in the offing!'

Jill didn't reflect for long. It would be

childish to hide away. 'Right, I'll get my jacket.'

Everyone made an effort to make the meal a pleasant affair. After Jill heard some considerate comments and understanding remarks about being scared of heights, the episode was more or less ignored. The conversation became quite general. They ate a delicious meal of chicken in a creamy sauce with baked potatoes and green salad.

By the time they'd reached the delicious trifle, everyone, including Jill, was completely relaxed and looking forward to their walk next day. Everyone was also complaining about sore muscles. They sat around for a while, playing cards or darts or just watching television until they gradually drifted off to their rooms to sleep.

★   ★   ★

When Jill rose, she looked out of the window. Yesterday there had been fog at this time of day, but today there was none and the sky was clear. She sighed in pleasurable anticipation.

The day started leisurely, with plenty of time for everyone to sleep longer if they wished, or to dawdle over breakfast. Once all five participants were ready, Danny fetched the van. They all poured inside and Jill watched the passing scenery as they sped onwards. The sun was shining and it was the loveliest time of the year. They passed hedges of white hawthorn, fields dotted with buttercups and daisies, green budding trees and fresh burgeoning grass. The van climbed the terrain and stopped at the nature reserve visitors' centre.

Danny left them hoisting their rucksacks and went inside. A few minutes later, he returned with Blake Armand. 'You lot don't deserve it, but the chief warden himself is going to be your guide on this walk.'

The weekend group laughed and Jill joined in weakly. She hadn't expected to see him again — or for him to be in charge of the walk.

Blake looked the group over and met Jill's glance. He smiled, at no one in particular, and said, 'I'd like to show you some of my favourite spots around here. We'll walk for a couple of hours, take a break for lunch and come back by another route.' He glanced at their footwear. 'I see you all have sensible footwear, so there should be no problems — but I do always carry plasters in my pack if you need one! If my pace is too fast, don't hesitate to tell me.

'If you're ready, we'll head off through that field over there. It goes without saying that we stick to the paths, wherever they exist, close any gates behind us, and try not to disturb plants or animals on the way.'

Jill joined the end of the group and watched as the others clustered around Blake and began to chat to him as he moved forward with purposeful strides. Sometimes she saw his face when he turned to talk to someone nearby. His smile was sudden and arresting.

She conceded he was definitely not the dour character she'd labelled him to be at first. He was a dynamic, dependable man who took his job seriously. His action in taking her down from halfway up the fissure was an instinctive response to a difficult situation, and it was done with skill. People liked him; the way they wanted to stay near him proved that. She walked steadily at the rear of the group, and resolved to enjoy the day.

They followed a narrow lane that turned right and uphill, passed through a gate and went through a small wood at a steady pace. Blake explained it was a protected area because of its extensive bird life. The track was churned up in places by forestry vehicles, and Jill wondered idly what the birds thought about that.

Once out of the wood, they crossed over bogland, following paths that were barely distinguishable. Ascending a hill, they eventually reached the summit, where there was no shelter and little vegetation. The ridge walk was pleasant despite a stiff breeze and the glimpses of the valley below were tantalising in the sunlight. Ahead of her, the sunlight found Blake's glossy dark hair and glinted, making it look like dark, polished marble.

When they reached a cluster of boulders, Blake called, 'Halt! We'll have a break here.'

No one protested, and out came the sandwiches and flasks of tea.

Jill moved to a nearby rock and made herself comfortable. She squatted like a leprechaun, munched contentedly on her sandwiches and viewed the terrain below. There was a wonderful feeling of space all around that reminded her of her dad's farm.

Blake came across to join her. Immediately she tensed and felt her pulse accelerate, but she strove to appear unconcerned. He had a cup of coffee in his hand, and placed his foot against the rock.

'We haven't had a chance to talk until now. Everything okay — after yesterday?'

As casually as she could manage, she replied, 'Yes, thank you — I slept like a log and I'm enjoying myself this morning.'

'You look like it. You obviously walk more often than you climb rocks.' There was a touch of amusement in his eyes.

Confused by her agitation, and wondering why Blake always seemed to have this effect on her, she replied rather more sharply than she had intended, 'My parents have a sheep farm. I'm used to walking long distances, even if I'm out of practice!'

His eyebrows lifted and his firm mouth curled as if it was on the edge of laughter. 'You're a farmer's daughter? Hard to believe, when I think how you normally dress and look!'

She finished her sandwich, brushed her hands free of crumbs and crossed her arms across her slight frame, fixing him with her green eyes. 'And why

81

shouldn't farmers' daughters be stylish? We're not living in the Dark Ages any more.' The breeze blew her hair across her face and she shoved it determinedly behind her ears again.

He viewed her with amusement. 'You're right — why not indeed!' He threw the remainder of his cold coffee in an arc into the nearby bracken and looked at his watch. 'We'd better get going if we are to be back by the stated time. Most people have to get home tonight.' He paused. 'You too?'

She eyed him cautiously. 'No, I'm going to see if there's a free room for the night in the Owens's pub. I have the day off tomorrow, so I can afford to go home in stages.'

He nodded, and turned to the others. 'Time to go, everyone! Take your rubbish with you!'

They followed Blake as he led them straight down towards a sheep-dip near a river. Jill didn't catch all the information he gave them as they went — she made no special effort to stay close to him. He was never alone, and the others clearly felt comfortable in his company so he was doing a good job. Jill heard them all laugh about something he said from time to time.

She wished she could overcome her reluctance to seek him out; he was only a man like any other, wasn't he?

They crossed the river and followed a faint, narrow path that veered to the left. The weather remained fine, and the rest of the way was easy on the feet and over flat ground. They reached the visitor's centre on time.

The van was waiting for them, and Sharon Burton came out of the centre to meet the party. Everyone was thoroughly satisfied with the day's walk, and although a couple of people claimed to be worn out, they all agreed they'd had a good time. Everyone thanked Blake, and Jill nodded too and joined the clapping to show their appreciation before heading for the van that would take them back to the activity centre.

As she was waiting to climb in, she heard Sharon talking to him insistently. 'Think it over, Blake. I've heard the cooking is excellent. I'm sure you'd enjoy a good meal, and as I'm inviting you, it'll be for free!'

Jill was glad to bundle herself into the van and not listen to their conversation. A few minutes later, they were on their way, and she stared determinedly out of the window. Blake, standing in the entrance porch, waved to the van as it accelerated down the road.

* * *

In some ways, Jill was glad to be alone again, even though the members of the course had been a good bunch — and, apart from the climbing scare, she'd enjoyed the weekend. She resolved to do more walking, whenever she could. Perhaps she could persuade one of her friends to come with her; walking any distance alone wouldn't be sensible, or much fun.

She drove back along the coast road, and when she passed Jack's cottage her thoughts wandered to Coomer Island. She'd be coming back to show Clyde Chapman around at the end of the week, and she hadn't been to Coomer since the end of last year.

She stopped and fumbled through the collection of papers in the glove compartment until she found the tide table. It was low tide at present, and she had more than an hour before she'd need to be back on firm land again. She parked the car on the side of the main road, covering the short distance to the banking quickly. She strode across the damp shingle and shiny rocks towards the jetty.

Once on the island, it was still warm enough to enjoy a brief walk. Everything looked much greener and more cheerful than on her last visit. She noticed that there was a lot more noise from various birds singing and calling before they settled for the night. She was careful to walk in the open sections of the land as much as possible — hoping to cause less alarm among the nesting birds by doing so.

She ended up in the small cove, and stared out to sea. The remaining sunlight was glistening like silver coins on the surface of the greyish water. Protected from most of the sea breezes in the bay, she lay back on one of the rocks and closed her eyes.

★ ★ ★

She woke, startled by the knowledge she'd fallen asleep. It couldn't have been for long, but she realised before she checked her wristwatch that the high tide was in full swing by now — and spring tides were always fast and quick-flowing. Any attempt to cross back to the mainland would be a foolhardy undertaking.

After a short period of panic following the realisation that she was stuck on the island for roughly seven hours, Jill began thinking about how she would cope. There wasn't any point in rushing back and fore to the jetty; it was better to use the time more sensibly — because daylight was beginning to fade. No one knew she was here. She had her mobile phone, but didn't have Jack Lewis' phone number — nor that of the pub.

At least she'd be able to bunk down in the house. Glad that she had somewhere to shelter from the wind and the worst of the cold, she started back up the slope to the building. The fiery remains of the setting sun were reflected in the windows, and at this moment it was a welcoming sanctuary.

She found the key safe under its stone, and on closer inspection of the downstairs rooms she discovered an old-fashioned cast-iron stove in the living room that she hadn't noticed before. She only hoped no birds had blocked the chimney with their nests. Blake Armand's coffee equipment was spread out on some old newspapers on the bogus Welsh dresser.

She needed water to make something to drink, and wood to make a fire.

Grabbing the small kettle and some used plastic bottles, she searched for the well around the side of the house. Once she found it, she wrestled with the pulley and winched up a battered bucket with water. Swilling and emptying the bucket, kettle and bottles several times, she then filled them and dumped them in the kitchen. Daylight was fading fast as she began to search the area for deadwood.

It was a time-consuming task and the outcome was sobering. When she piled the wood next to the fireplace, it was only a modest stack. She knew there were matches next to Blake's gas burner in the kitchen; there was newspaper under the coffee things, and she had an office organiser in her rucksack, but they were her only sources of paper. She was reluctant to use her organiser for lighting a fire, but if all else failed she'd have to sacrifice it. All important future appointments were already stored in her computer in the office, in any case.

She searched the immediate area again for more wood, but it was getting harder to see anything properly any more, so she came inside and shut the front door. She knelt in front of the old-fashioned stove and started to heap the smaller bits of wood on top of some of the paper; she decided to wait a while before lighting it. She'd probably feel the cold most of all in the small hours of the morning — no point in using all the wood up now — although a cheerful fire would have not only given some light, it would also have lifted her spirits no end.

Feeling around for the covered armchair, she was grateful for the sparse light still coming through the window and tried to make herself comfortable. However she was jolted out of her deliberations when she heard the sound of the heavy, damp-swollen front door dragging against the floor as someone pushed it open.

For a moment she was shocked and paralysed. All kinds of unpleasant thoughts shot through her brain in a matter of seconds. Who or what wandered around Coomer at this time of the day — was it ghosts, drug addicts, murderers, escaped prisoners? Her mouth was dry; her heart hammered so loud and so fast that she was sure it must be audible to anyone else. A click-clack, click-clack drifted down the hallway towards the sitting room, and close behind it were muffled, heavier treads.

Jill slipped to her knees and searched carefully and silently in the semi-darkness for a fire poker she'd noticed in the hearth. She was scared stiff, but a little more confident once she had taken silent hold of the iron poker and edged round the chair, along the wall to position herself behind the door. She lifted the poker, froze, and black fright overtook her feelings.

The door slowly edged open. When something wet touched her hand a few seconds later, she screamed softly, dropping the poker. It jangled and clattered loudly as it hit the floor.

Almost instinctively, Jill realised it must be Blake's dog Laurence. He jumped up against her chest and licked her chin, but fright was still in control of her senses. It was impossible to steady her erratic pulse. She took a deep breath as the door opened wider. The beams from a flashlight swept the room and rested on her as she sank slowly to her knees.

Hugging the warm, slightly damp Laurence, she buried her face in his shaggy fur for a second or two, in an attempt to give herself time to recover.

She looked into the torchlight, unable to see the man holding it, but knew it could only be him. 'Blake? Do you realise you just gave me the biggest shock of my life? How could you creep up on me like that, without proper warning? Why didn't you shout?'

He chortled in the dark and the chortle turned into a belly laugh.

Slowly she was recovering, and she took a deep, shaky breath. 'Do you mind turning that torch in another direction? How can you be so brainless?'

Still laughing, he did what she asked and had the grace to apologise. 'Sorry, I didn't think about the fact that I might scare you — but if you could only see your face!' He spluttered in his attempt to control his amusement.

'It is not funny! I thought you were a ghost, or a killer, or someone with nasty intentions. I must have aged ten years just now! So what are you doing here?'

'Same as you, I expect — I've been caught by the tide. I came across because I saw your car parked on the verge when I was on my way home. I wondered if you'd forgotten the time. The tide was rising fast when I crossed, and I can assure you that Laurence didn't enjoy wading across up to his chest in the water, but he was the one who insisted we came, to make sure you were all right. We walked around to make sure you weren't lying somewhere injured and, when there was no sign of you anywhere else, I decided you must be in here.'

It was a bit eerie talking to him by the sparse light of his torch directed towards the ceiling, but now that she was adjusting, his solid presence suddenly made her feel a whole lot better — even though she didn't want to admit that to him. His face was half-covered by shadows. She tried to relax.

'I've been making preparations for a fire.'

'Good idea! You've got wood?'

She gestured. 'Not much, I'm afraid. I didn't have much time to collect any more.'

He came across and she could now look up into his face, even though his features still were etched with shadows. He glanced down at the hearth.

'That won't last long, and most of it is probably damp! I think there are some proper logs piled against the wall out in the shed.'

Jill wished she'd thought of looking there.

'Let's go and get some. If you hold the torch, I'll carry.' He turned away and Jill had no choice but to follow.

She helped to carry a couple of logs with one arm as she illuminated their way back and forth. After a couple of journeys, they had a sizeable pile of logs next to the fireplace and a cheerful fire burning in the grate.

She held her hands to the flames. 'That's better!' She hesitated, but finally managed to say, 'Thanks for coming.'

They dragged the sofa in front of the fireplace and merged their supplies. Jill had a bar of chocolate, an apple, and a packet of crisps in her rucksack, and Blake had a sandwich, a roll of peppermints, a couple of dog biscuits, and some cubes of cheese. They surveyed their booty and eyed each other.

Blake volunteered, 'There's a tin of

biscuits in the kitchen too — it's not full, but I think there are still a few left.'

'Really? Good! How hungry are you?'

'What do you think? I'm always hungry, almost as bad as Laurence.'

'Oh! Well, Laurence can have the dog biscuits; I think we're agreed on that, aren't we? Actually, I tried eating dog biscuits once; they're not nearly as bad as I expected. When we were small, my brothers dared me, and of course I had to have a go.'

With dry amusement in his voice, he agreed. 'Okay — the dog biscuits for Laurence!'

'You can have the sandwich — it's yours anyway. If you don't mind, I'll have the cheese, and we share all the rest, okay? There'll be nothing left for breakfast, but we'll be able to cross by six-thirty.'

Fun flickered in the eyes that met hers by the light of the flames from the logs burning in the grate. 'Fine! I'll get the biscuit tin, and make us a cup of coffee when I'm there. Where's the torch? Do you want milk and sugar?'

'Where do we get milk from?'

'You probably didn't notice, but there's a jar of powdered milk. I don't like it black.'

'Lovely! Milk and a spoonful of sugar for me then, please.'

★   ★   ★

If Blake was still hungry, he didn't complain and didn't show it. Jill would gladly have given him her share — she wasn't very hungry, but she knew he wouldn't have accepted, so she didn't try. They were munching away at the remaining biscuits, and the roll of peppermints was still lying comfortably between them. It was a long couch, but now and then Blake's thigh touched hers as he moved about or leaned back, and when it happened her mind unaccountably froze for several moments.

They stared into the flames; Laurence was stretched out sleeping at their feet, his jaws twitching faintly now and then, and his tail too.

She was too curious not to use the chance to ask about his life. 'Have you always been a warden?'

'No. After university I worked in a bank. I wasn't particularly happy there, but the money was good, and I thought it was enough to build a future on.'

'But it wasn't?'

'At that time I thought I was seriously in love, but then I found out that was a great mistake.'

'Oh . . . I'm sorry.' Jill was disconcerted at his frankness. 'I wasn't meaning to pry into your private life.'

He leaned forward towards the flames; the light danced on the aesthetic lines of his face. 'I know that, otherwise I wouldn't have told you. Actually I'm glad things turned out as they did, because I now realise we weren't at all suited. She was someone who wanted the so-called good life, and she measured everything by whether it had a brand name, whether it would mean a step upwards on the social ladder, and whether it would win her more recognition.'

He shrugged. 'I always had my problems with that, but I toed the line, because I wanted to be in love with her. She was clever and beautiful.' He shifted and continued. 'Someone else caught her eye. Someone who was further up the career ladder — with more connections and better prospects — and they got married.'

'And then?'

'Then I started to think about what I wanted to do with the rest of my life. I was sure I wanted to get out of the rat race, but it was mere chance that led me to do some voluntary work with the British Conservation Trust. That led to a part-time job for six months, and after various courses I qualified in country-side management and eventually ended up where I am.'

'And you like it better, what you do for a living now?' she asked him.

'I love it. There couldn't be a better sort of life for me. I don't earn as much, but I have enough for my needs.'

Decisively she responded, 'Good! It was brave of you to do something that was so different — changing course mid-stream, as they say. I think lots of people know they are in the wrong kind of slot, but cling on until it's too late to change anything.'

'Perhaps that's why I enjoy my job; because I found out what was wrong early enough to do something about it. I was always interested in the country-side and animals, and I'm now prepared to do whatever I can to preserve all the things we've been given free. If ever I saw Anne again, I'd thank her for stopping me making the biggest mistake of my life. If we had paired up, I'd probably be divorced by now, but still be working in an environment that I basically hated.'

He straightened his shoulders. 'And you? Do you like your job?'

'Yes, I do. I know you might not approve of what I do . . . ' He shrugged, and she continued, 'But it does give me satisfaction to link people with exactly the home they're looking for. Not everyone is loaded with money, and I really try to give people the very best value for what they can afford. I don't worry so much about the financial side when I'm working for companies, or people who are loaded with money, but I still do my best to find them what they want.'

'You make dreams come true?'

She glanced at him and smiled. 'In a sense, I suppose I do — or rather, I try to do that.'

'And personally — what about a boyfriend, partner, companion?'

'Not at the moment. It's not so easy to find the right person, is it?'

He fumbled around in his rucksack on the side of the couch and brought out a small CD player. A mixture of swing, jazz and classical music was soon filling the background silences.

She smiled warmly at him again. 'Great! I must say, this is turning into a very comfortable evening with good company.' Her heart skipped, realising what she had said.

'I've spent worse evenings, too. What about the music? Okay with you?'

She nodded. 'I'm flexible, music-wise, and I must admit we seem to have similar tastes.'

They talked about people in the village, the activity centre (although Jill avoided mentioning Sharon Burton's name), and he told her a little about the kind of activities the nature reserve's visitor's centre offered all year round, and snippets about his family background. Jill didn't feel compelled to talk continually, and there were quiet intervals when they both listened to the crackling of the fire and the sound of the music, although their minds were busy with other thoughts. There was no running water in the house so when she went outside to go to the toilet, Blake sent Laurence along, and gave her the torch. Laurence was quite happy to go with her.

It was soon warm enough in the

room to feel comfortable and Jill's eyes grew heavy. Ultimately, she fell asleep, and she slid gradually sideways until she came to rest against his body. Blake looked down at her, noticing how her dark lashes fanned out delicately over her cheeks. He smiled gently and put his arm around her sleeping figure.

Unaware, she slept on. She didn't even stir when he changed his position from time to time so that he could renew the logs in the grate.

★   ★   ★

Dawn had hardly begun when Jill woke. Very faint daylight was fighting its way through the dirty windows. She was curled up on the couch with Blake's coat draped over her. The fire was burning brightly. She sat up, tried to straighten out the cricks in her neck and shoulders, and was wondering where he was when she heard the door open. Laurence's noisier entrance heralded Blake's return. His tail wagged

102

furiously when he saw she was awake at last. She stood up, yawned and was stretching as Blake came in.

'Morning! Where have you been? Thanks for your coat — but you should have taken it, especially if you've been wandering around outside.'

'It's not cold, and I only went as far as the cove to see what the day was going to be like, and to give Laurence a chance to explore.'

She was acutely aware of him, of his lean, athletic figure. To distract herself she leaned down to stroke the dog's head.

'Isn't Laurence ever tempted to chase the birds?'

He smiled. His hair had been ruffled by the breeze and his face was shadowed by the beginnings of a beard.

'He probably is, but he knows it's more than his life's worth to try anything, so he just watches them — rather wistfully. I came up to get you.'

He held out his hand. She automatically put hers in his and followed him down the corridor. She felt a ripple of excitement, and told herself not to be stupid — she liked him, but that was all, even though the pull seemed to be getting stronger each time she saw him.

They wandered down the slope and he let go of her hand as they neared the cove. He gestured to Laurence to lie down and he obeyed. Blake looked at Jill, put his finger to his lips and pointed.

On one of the flatter rocks lay a seal with its eyes closed, enjoying the solitude. It opened its eyes, measured the two of them, and decided these humans presented no immediate danger, so it turned on its back and leisurely scratched itself. Jill noticed that its stomach was spotted and paler than its back. She'd never been so close to a wild seal before.

After a while, the creature made its cumbersome way back into the water and dived. She watched it heading out to sea beyond the headline rocks.

'What a way to start the day! Do seals come here regularly?'

'Probably, but I don't come that often myself — only to check things generally, or if something needs attention. I've seen them here several times, so they may be using it as a safe haven.' He looked at his watch. 'By the time we've had coffee and sorted things up at the house, we'll be able to cross.' He rubbed his hands across his roughened chin. 'I could do with a shower, a shave and a good breakfast.' He started up the slope again.

Jill stood for a moment. It was still dawn; the air was misty, cool winds were blowing from the sea, and the waves were hissing and chuckling as they hit the rocks. It was a place for being, rather than doing.

Reluctantly she turned and followed him towards the house.

★　★　★

Blake's car was parked near hers.

'Thanks again!' she said brightly. 'It would have been a lot trickier spending a night on the island without you.'

He waved her thanks aside. 'I suppose you won't stay at the pub now?'

She shook her head. 'No, I may as well drive straight home.'

He nodded. 'I'll do the same.'

'I'm back here again at the end of the week, though — Clyde Chapman has shown some interest, and I've arranged to take him across and show him around on Friday afternoon.'

His brows drew together into a frown. 'Clyde Chapman the pop singer?'

Jill was surprised he knew the name. 'Yes.' She wrapped a scarf that had freed itself and was blowing in the wind, more tightly round her neck.

He stiffened, and his expression hardened. 'Oh Lord! Imagine what that might mean for the wildlife over there.'

Jill understood his reaction, but couldn't alter the situation, so she didn't comment. She crouched in front of Laurence and kissed his silky head. 'Take care, my friend, and don't give in to temptation.'

Laurence seemed to grin up at her and his eyes shone like black buttons.

Blake whistled to him. 'Come on, Laurence!' He viewed Jill and said. 'Sometimes I wish I was a dog — it's not a bad life, most of the time.' He opened the door of his Land Rover and Laurence jumped in the back. The Mini followed the bigger car the short distance to the main road, and then they drove off in opposite directions.

5

Clyde Chapman was in his mid-twenties. He was as thin as a pencil, with curly blond hair and inquisitive blue eyes. Each of his ears displayed a row of silver rings, and there was a tattoo with a Chinese symbol on the side of his neck. His clothes looked like items from Oxfam's bargain box, but he was clean and acted like a normal human being. Jill hadn't known what to expect, even wondering if he'd turn up under the influence of drugs or alcohol. His manager was in his fifties and dressed conservatively in jeans, a polo shirt and a short leather jacket.

Jack Lewis ferried them all across to Coomer. Jill had no doubt that it would soon be public knowledge that the prospective owner of Coomer Island was a wacky pop star.

Clyde, his manager and Jill wandered

around a bit, and Jill let them talk to one another about what they saw without commenting. She guided them gradually towards the cove.

Once there, Clyde looked around and nodded. 'Hey, this is a good spot! Plenty of room to have a session and a bit of a jamboree on the beach.'

Jill winced as she thought about the wildlife.

Tom, Clyde's manager, looked sceptical. 'I wouldn't come down here in the summer — not even for one of your parties! An English summer would freeze people's backsides off!'

Clyde looked towards the house. The slope was covered in dandelions. 'It may not be California or Mallorca, but it does have possibilities!'

'Does it? You're welcome to it; it's your money. I've told you before — if you want something local, you'd be better off with a big house with lots of surrounding land.'

Jill recollected that she was here to try to sell this island. 'You wouldn't have the privacy on land like you have here. When the tide is in, you're cut off and no one would be stupid enough to try to swim across. You could get some kind of barrier constructed to stop anyone using the jetty the rest of the time. It's almost impossible to land elsewhere. They would be mad to land on the mud banks, and fight their way through the wilderness. The house isn't big, but it's ideal as a weekend hideaway. Once modernised, it'd be perfect!'

Clyde stuck his thumbs in his pockets and nodded. 'Let's have a look at the house. My girlfriend has the last word, but I wanted to have a look around first — to see whether it's worth her making the trip.'

They set off, up the slope. Jill asked. 'Is your girlfriend local too? You come from this area, don't you?'

'Yep! Lynette keeps my feet on the ground. I'd be flying a kite every day if it wasn't for her — she's my life jacket. We've been together since we were fifteen. We'd have married years ago, if it wasn't for the publicity factor. You know how female fans hate stars to be married! We will, one day, though. She supported me when no one else believed in the band, and she kept me on the straight and narrow.'

Jill reflected that there was more to this man than she'd first imagined. They reached the porch and she opened the door. 'Perhaps you'd like to look around on your own? Kitchen, dining room and sitting room down-stairs, three bedrooms and a bathroom upstairs.'

The two men ambled away, and Jill wandered into the sitting room. The sofa was still in front of the fireplace, and there was a smell of burnt wood. The fire the other day seemed to have done the room some good — it no longer smelt so musty and unused. She stood by the window, next to the shabby curtains, and looked down at the cove and the grey sea beyond.

The weather was good today; the sun

was shining weakly, and even if the waves were jerky and rough, the overall impression was a good one — a lot better than the first day she'd come here. Deep down she didn't want to think about how radically it would change if someone like Clyde took over. The seals would have to look for another quiet spot to visit, most of the birds would relocate their nesting places, and the animals would probably escape to the mainland. She told herself it was none of her business.

The men's voices echoed as they wandered around. Eventually they joined her again.

Clyde said, 'The rooms are too small. I expected something bigger — like a Victorian mansion. It would have to be gutted to make it habitable. What about extending, building on, installing an outside swimming pool, that sort of thing?'

Jill shrugged. 'To be honest — I should imagine that will be difficult, if not impossible. The island is a designated place of Special Scientific Interest.'

Tom asked, 'What does that mean?'

'You'll have to get expert advice, but roughly I think it means you are restricted in what you can change or alter. That's why the conservation people had a lease on the land up until now; they didn't want to change anything and have let it run wild. The family who own it didn't want to use it themselves, and it can't be sold for commercial purposes. If you bought the island, you would be able to modernise the house, and I presume you could tame the land directly adjacent to the house, but anything else would be debatable. You can modernise as much as you like in the house as long as the external appearance isn't changed.'

She tried to sound encouraging. 'The sitting room and dining room combined would make a lovely room, overlooking the cove. The kitchen is a decent size. Knock the two smaller bedrooms into one, and put in a new bathroom. It would suffice for a holiday home. You'd have to be careful about altering anything else.' She noticed their startled expressions. 'It's my job to point out the disadvantages, as well as the advantages. I wouldn't want you to buy something and be mad with our firm afterwards because we didn't explain the situation properly.'

'What's your name?'

'Jill.'

'Well, Jill — If the wilderness near here was cleared, the house modernised and the weather was good enough, it might be an interesting investment, but I'll have to talk to Lynette. If she wants to come for a look, I'll be in touch again.'

'Of course. There are photos in that file I gave you, but I'll be pleased to show you, or her, or both of you around again any time.'

Jill phoned Jack and asked him to pick them up. The men walked down to the cove to wait. Tom was smoking, and she winced when she saw him flick his dog-end between the rocks. She called them when she saw Jack cruising up the coast, ready to turn and come in on the far side. The path to the jetty was firm now, if overgrown with pale green stems of fems.

They disembarked close to the parked cars and Jill paid Jack discreetly before he tipped his cap and pushed off into the narrow channel again. The two men followed her back to their cars and she shook hands with them both. She'd revised her preconceptions about Clyde Chapman. She thought he'd be a chaotic anarchist, dependent on drugs or alcohol; he was perfectly normal, as were his reactions. His celebrity status might require an outward show of rebellious behaviour, but his private life was another thing.

'If you need any more information, don't hesitate to get in touch. You have my folder, and there are extra descriptions and photos in there. Have a safe journey and I hope to hear from you sometime.'

Clyde was turning away; the sunshine caught his earrings. He grinned and lifted his hand. 'Thanks, babe! I'll let you know!'

Someone coming down the gravel path interrupted them, and they all looked up. Jill was flummoxed to see it was Blake. He came at a determined pace and glanced briefly in Jill's direction before he concentrated on the other two men. He clearly knew Clyde Chapman because he addressed the right person.

'Mr Chapman, can I have a word with you — about Coomer Island? My name is Blake Armand, and I'm the warden of the nearby conservation area. Until now, we leased Coomer Island from its owners. I won't delay you, but I want to tell you something about the island and what I think will happen if inroads are made into the habits of the wildlife in and around the island. You will already know it is classified as a place of Special Scientific Interest, and I have to warn you we'll fight any proposals to change the island, whoever buys it.'

Tom was about to block any further

conversation, but Clyde caught hold of his arm and he nodded in Blake's direction. 'Tell me more!'

Jill's mouth was half-open. Blake was the last person she'd expected to see here today. He had no right to butt in on her meeting with a client. He was trying to influence negotiations — even warning Clyde off. He was sabotaging her efforts to do her job. It was so unexpected and so unfair of him! She wanted to complain but it was counter-productive to have a quarrel with anyone in front of clients. It was too late to stop him now.

Her expression clouded in anger and she gave him a hostile glare, which he chose to ignore. Her anger increased. It was brass neck impertinence. He'd used her to find out when Clyde Chapman was viewing — and then set out to use it for his own purpose. She wasn't angry that he wanted to find a way to protect Coomer — that was understandable — but because he'd exploited her.

Her breath burned in her throat and

she felt a sense of loss. She'd thought he liked her, but she'd misjudged him. She'd been a means to an end. Without another word, she turned and hurried along the gravel track to her Mini. She'd already said goodbye to Clyde Chapman and his manager, so she wasn't being impolite. The wheels spun and gravel shot to the sides as she accelerated and drove off.

★ ★ ★

'I don't want to talk to him, Clive. Tell him I'm out, gone shopping, on leave, gone to the moon, whatever you like.'

Clive tilted his head to the side and viewed her speculatively. 'This isn't the first time he's called. He's a determined character. He asked for your telephone number or your address, but I refused, of course.'

'He can stand on his head for all I care — I don't want to talk to him, full stop!' She picked up a folder and went towards John's office, knocked and went in. 'Here's the contract with all the details for that house in Hill Street.'

He held out his hand and took it. 'Ripping! Another one off the list. You've done well this week; this is the third one, isn't it?'

She nodded. 'I was lucky. These people knew what they wanted, liked what they saw, and the house fitted their financial limits, so it went very smoothly. It's a very nice house, actually; lots of Georgian features. The original windows have been replaced by modern versions but otherwise it's been kept in good shape, considering it's roughly two hundred years old.'

'I must admit I feel attracted to Georgian buildings myself. I like the symmetry, the fanlights, and all the rest. They fit the era so beautifully. Just think of those Regency rags — the gloves, the tight pants, the fob watches!'

She smiled at him. 'Born too late, eh, John? I bet you would have enjoyed parading around like Beau Brummell, wouldn't you?'

He grinned. 'Rather! What about that island? Any response?'

Jill had already told him about Blake barging in on her viewing. She shook her head. 'Not so far. I haven't tried to push things yet — but we'll have to find out if he has decided one way or the other. I'll give it a couple more days, and then phone his manager. I shouldn't have told Blake Armand that he'd be there on that Friday afternoon.'

John looked at her speculatively, shuffled the papers on his desk and looked up at her again. 'Anything going on between you two?'

Jill tried to look bland and unconcerned. 'No, of course not. I met him briefly on Coomer the first time I visited it, but he wasn't very welcoming, and I met him again on the activity weekend course. I should have been more careful and less friendly. He's not my type.'

John noticed her heightened colour, but had enough sensitivity not to force any more information out of her.

'These things happen. Don't worry too much. Some you win, some you lose, and it wasn't an easy item to move from the beginning, was it? We both know that. Keep pounding away; perhaps we'll find someone else if Clyde throws in the towel.'

Jill was still printing out information and preparing for the next day's appointments after her colleagues had left. They all had keys, so there was never a problem if someone worked late, or came in early. She heard the outer door open and took her pencil from behind her ear. She straightened her skirt, adjusted her red sweater, and went to the reception area. Her high heels echoed on the parquet floor as she walked. John should have locked the main door when he left, but he'd forgotten again.

'I'm sorry, we've closed for the day. Perhaps you can call tomorrow . . . ?' Her voice petered out when she saw Blake standing there. She swallowed hard, lifted her chin, and boldly met his gaze. 'What do you want?'

He hesitated, measuring her for a moment. 'I want to explain.'

The air was heavy with censure. She tried to project an ease she didn't feel. Studying the lean face, despite her attempts to remain cool and unmoved, his nearness made her senses spin. How could she be attracted to someone who had manipulated her trust and friendship?

Finally, she crossed her arms on her chest. Her face was pale. 'There's nothing to explain — you used confidential information you got from me to further your own scheme. You double-dealt me, Blake.'

He ran his hand over his face and then held out his hand in an entreating gesture. 'I know it is hard to understand, but I had to do whatever I could to try to save Coomer. I swear it wasn't my intention to mess up your talks. I was merely in the vicinity on Friday afternoon and suddenly remembered what you told me about Chapman coming. My instincts told me it was my one chance to present our position before he decided one way or the other. If you got into trouble with your boss, I'll talk to him and take full responsibility!'

Her ironic tone belied her turbulent emotions. 'How noble! How very kind!' Her lips were a thin line. 'Trouble is, I don't believe you regret your interference. It was wrong of you; full stop!'

He spoke with desperate but quiet determination. 'I don't regret trying to save Coomer. I do regret that you were caught in the crossfire, and I'm sorry if it has harmed our friendship.'

'Friendship? You don't know the meaning of the word, *Mr* Armand. No friend of mine has ever made use of me like that before. It's taught me a lesson! If you'll excuse me, I have work to do and it's already late.' She struggled to maintain an even tone.

A muscled clenched in his jaw and his features hardened.

Jill gave him no chance to respond.

She turned on her heel, walked quickly back down the short corridor to her office cubicle and slammed the door. She sat down at her desk and stared at the computer screen without seeing it. She heard the outer office door closing and knew she was alone again. She clasped her hands tightly as she sat in lonely silence. What she saw as Blake's betrayal had hit her very hard, and she felt an inexplicable emptiness. She told herself she would be glad if she never saw him again.

* * *

Jill received a voucher for a day's activity course of her choice, with a short letter from Sharon Burton apologising again for putting her in an uncomfortable situation. Jill shoved it into a drawer and forgot about it. She did not intend to visit the centre again.

Finally, Clyde Chapman's manager phoned her, and after a minute or two of chitchat, he told her that Clyde had decided to buy the island. For a couple of seconds she was speechless. Knowing that Clyde was in a position to choose a more eye-catching property in a milder climate, and that Blake Armand had undoubtedly tried to make the island an unattractive prospect for anyone to buy, she was bewildered.

She found her voice. 'That's great news.' She hesitated before she added, 'I honestly thought it wasn't what he was looking for — especially after he'd seen the house.'

Tom laughed. 'As far as I'm concerned the place is only good as a combat training area. You need a compass, or you'll get lost in the wilderness. I advised him against it, but he's quite determined. I don't understand why, but it won't be a drain on his money. He just needs to play one extra gig and he'll have the price in the bag.'

Jill swallowed hard. It was a lot of money as far as she was concerned — but she didn't earn a fortune by jumping around on a stage and blasting peoples' eardrums. 'Doesn't Clyde's girlfriend want to see it? I thought he never made any serious decisions without her?'

'That's very true! Actually, they've already been back together and had another look around.'

'Oh!' Jill was startled at this news.

'He told me yesterday he was going to buy it, and that I should set the wheels in motion. You'll need to get this all sorted out before he sets out on his next world tour. If it means lots of paperwork — you'd better get going, sweetheart, because if you don't, you may have to wait a long time before you can pin him down again.'

'Yes . . . yes. I'll tell the present owners about his offer straight away, I'm sure they'll accept. You'll need a solicitor to act for you. He or she has to contact the seller's solicitor requesting title deeds to the property and initiate contract negotiations; after that you will be ready to exchange contracts and agree a date for completion. Between exchange and completion, you transfer the amount into your solicitor's account, and he transfers it to the seller's solicitor on completion day. Your solicitor pays stamp duty on your behalf. I can send you a summary of what's to do, if you like.'

'No need! We went through the same kind of rigmarole a while back, when he bought his London house.' He was scribbling away. 'I'll send you the necessary details about his lawyer in an email straight away.'

'Well — thanks, Tom. Please tell Clyde that if he wants to take another look around any time, just let me know.'

'Can't imagine he will, but will do, honey!'

'There was a click and the connection was cut. She should have been whooping that the island was off their hands, but for some reason she could only think about how Blake would feel when he found out that all his efforts had been in vain. He'd tried hard to influence Clyde that Friday afternoon in the hope of saving the island for the wildlife and nature.

She felt angry about how he took advantage of the situation, but she also knew he was just as serious about his job as she was about hers.

6

A couple of weeks later John tapped the glass and motioned to Jill to come into his office. 'Take a seat before you fall over!' he urged.

'Why? What's happened?'

'Read this!' He handed her an email. She glanced at the name of the sender and read on.

John heard her quick intake of breath and remarked, 'It's amazing, eh!'

She was stunned. 'Clyde bought it, and is going to hand it over to the conservation authorities?'

'Yep! It goes to show there must be more inside that head than just tattoo ink and cotton wool.'

The print-out lay on her lap. She stared wordlessly across the desk.

John leaned back in his chair and played with a gold-capped pen. 'It's not often that you get the chance to express an undivided good opinion about today's youngsters, but Clyde caps it all. Fancy laying out all that hard cash, just to hand it over to someone else.'

'It's staggering! Good for him!'

'He'll get a lot of positive publicity, of course — so it's not all money down the drain — but he could have got plenty of other kinds of publicity for far less than Coomer's selling price.'

Jill looked thoughtfully out of the window. 'Um! Clyde Chapman never fitted my preconceptions of what a rock star would be like. His appearance is a bit quirky, but he never acted oddly or like a diva when I was around. He seems to have hung on to the real world.

'I suspect it has a lot to do with his girlfriend. I haven't met her, but I got the impression that she influenced him strongly. He said they were childhood sweethearts and they both come from the vicinity of Coomer Island. I suspect they talked about it and decided it would be a good deed to give it to the conservation people.'

'Your boyfriend is going to be delighted when he hears about this unexpected development, isn't he?'

Jill coloured. 'If you're talking about Blake Armand, he's not my boyfriend. What gives you that idea?'

John shrugged. 'The impression I got when you talked about him. You were extremely angry when he came here after hours to make his peace and sent him packing with a flea in his ear. You are generally unflappable, so I decided there was more to it than met the eye. The vibrations were seismic. You're not indifferent about him — even if you pretend you are.'

Jill threw back her hair and tried to look unconcerned. Her green eyes sparkled with defiance. 'Don't be daft, I hardly know the man.'

'Even if you function like thunder and lightning together, you are still the same storm. There's no reason you can't still like him; he was only bent on doing his job, you can't blame him for

131

that. Re-evaluate the situation, calm down and let things drift. There's nothing wrong with him, apart from the fact he was too caught up in his job. Is that so wrong?'

She laughed half-heartedly. 'Perhaps not, but he could have torpedoed everything. My job is just as important to me as his is to him!'

John grinned. 'Fools rush in where angels fear to tread. I'm sure he wouldn't have done it, if he'd stopped to think about the after-effects.'

'Huh! You are the eternal romantic! We're not likely to see each other again, and even if we did, he has no reason to like me any more — that's if he ever did!' She got up, placing the email back on his desk. 'I am pleased that Coomer will remain a sanctuary for the birds and other animals. If you'd been there, I'm sure you'd agree.'

John looked horrified. 'Perhaps — but think of the wellies! Nothing would entice me to wear them!'

She smiled. 'A pair of sturdy shoes

for a crossing at low-tide would do the job just as well. You wouldn't even get the soles of your shoes wet.'

He smiled. 'I'll remember that, if fate ever sends me in that direction — and if the conservation people allow me to visit it, of course.'

She left him, and wandered back to her desk. She started organising the information about the premises of a shop she was taking a buyer around that afternoon — but her thoughts drifted constantly and she gave up. She went to the small kitchen for some coffee, cradled it in her hands and looked out of the window at the boring view of the adjoining alleyway. It was true, she was pleased for Blake — and knew exactly how delighted he'd feel when he heard the news.

* * *

The following Monday an invitation arrived, addressed to Jill and John. Clyde Chapman was officially handing over the ownership of the island to the conservation authorities at a small reception. As John's firm had been involved in selling it, they were warmly invited to attend the function.

John put it down on her desk and watched the changing expression on her face with interest. Jill was seldom nervous or uptight; right now, she looked both. She'd worked for him for several years. He liked her, and felt protective. He mused that for some reason this island and her encounters with that young warden had certainly put the cat among the pigeons — more than she was willing to acknowledge.

She considered. 'It's really nice of Clyde — but I don't think I'll go.'

'Why ever not?'

She floundered. 'Oh, I don't know. It's not my scene, I suppose — standing around wasting precious time just for a glass of wine.'

'My dear colleague, it is never, ever, a waste of time to stand around anywhere if you have a glass of wine in your hand

— unless of course, it's really rotten wine! How many hours are we damned to wait for prospective clients who don't turn up for an appointment, and can't even be bothered to excuse themselves? That's much worse! A warm room and circling trays of wine and titbits beat that any day — or even sitting in this office twiddling our thumbs waiting for a client to walk through the door!' He paused. 'This has something to do with that warden chap, hasn't it?'

Awkwardly she cleared her throat. 'No, of course not!' She saw his lively eyes twinkling. Her colour heightened and she doodled on the paper in front of her. 'Well . . . perhaps a bit.'

He thrust his hands into the pockets of his beige trousers and viewed her seriously. 'I understand why you got annoyed about him, but quite honestly, my dear, as far as I can tell he's a decent chap who was just trying to do his job. What he did wasn't acceptable — but looking at the situation from his point of view, it was justified! Why not come with me and bury the hatchet? It's not like you to bear a grudge!'

She avoided his glance. 'I wouldn't be surprised if he ignored me.'

'You are too good-looking for any man to ignore! Who knows; he may not be there and then you'll regret you didn't come to sip some cool Chablis or Chardonnay from crystal glasses — and all at someone else's expense! I promise if he's there, I won't desert you and leave you in the lions' den.'

Jill hadn't thought about the possibility that he might not be there — but that might be true. Often the top-level management of any company, or organisation, liked to hog the limelight on special occasions like this. The gift of an island was scarcely an everyday event, and Blake might be pushed into the background. She threw back her shoulders. John was right; it was silly to carry this chip on her shoulder about him. The past was the past; she might never meet him again. The notion gave her a feeling of emptiness, and she refused to consider and wonder why.

'Oh, all right! When is it?' And Jill began to mull over what to wear.

* * *

On the actual day, after trying on, and discarding, several possibilities she finally chose an Empire-line, cap-sleeve, cotton ikat print dress in shades of brown and mauve. It skimmed her slim figure and ended just above her knees — showing off her legs to perfection. She clipped her hair behind her ears, and her eyes sparkled like dark emeralds as she surveyed the finished result in the mirror. She told herself she would have taken just as much care for any other function — only deep down she knew she was lying. It had to do with the fact that Blake Armand might be there.

When she met John, his eyebrows lifted and he whistled. 'My, oh my! You always look good, but you are a sight for sore eyes this morning.'

She eyed his serious suit and blue tie and felt apprehensive. 'Am I over-dressed? I can easily pop home again and change into a suit.'

He held out his arm. 'Not on your life! Let's go!'

The reception was at a well-known hotel, and the press was in attendance. Even if Clyde was squandering a large amount of money to buy an island, and choosing not to end up as its owner, it was still a perfect opportunity for some publicity; Tom, his manager, would make sure of that.

The room was already crowded, and Clyde Chapman was at its very centre. Jill and John wove through the throng of people and finally reached him. Standing next to Clyde was a petite girl with jet-black hair and delicate features. She must be Lynette — and if Jill was not mistaken, she'd persuaded Clyde to buy the island and pass it on to the conservation board.

Jill smiled at Clyde, who gave her a

cheeky 'Hi babe!' He turned slightly and explained to Lynnette, 'This is the woman who sold us the island.'

Lynette eyed her and the beginning of a smile tipped the corners of her mouth. 'Hi there! Clyde told me about you.'

'And Clyde told me about you. I think it is an absolutely wonderful and generous gesture — giving Coomer to the conservation people.'

Clyde shrugged. 'We talked about it, and we decided if we buy a holiday home, it'll be somewhere warmer, won't it, Lyn?' He put his arms around Lynette and went on. 'But we still decided to buy it and pass it on, mainly because we come from round here, and also because your friend had some very convincing arguments.'

She coloured a deeper shade of pink. 'Mr Blake is no special friend of mine; I don't understand why people think so.'

He tilted his head to one side. 'Sure? From the way he wove your name into the conversation all the time, I thought you two were together!'

With heightened colour, she replied, 'Well, we aren't! This is my boss, John. He's a fan of yours!' Jill was glad of the chance to direct the conversation elsewhere.

Clyde clearly made a great impression on John. Even though he looked like a homeless person in his sagging jacket, washed-out T-shirt and drainpipe jeans, Clyde's personality shone through. He was laid-back with great self-confidence, humour and intelligence. His girlfriend, Lynette, was wearing neater, uncluttered black clothing and Clyde seemed quite besotted with her. Jill remembered how Clyde said Lynette had kept his feet on the ground, and she could believe it. Other pop singers might need alcohol or drugs; Clyde Chapman only needed Lynette. It seemed he'd appreciated her qualities and stuck with her despite all the temptations from fans, models, and money-chasers that came his way.

Clyde remarked, 'I was knocked for

six when they told me the place will now be called The Chapman Conservation Centre. Gobsmacking, eh?'

Jill smiled. 'What a good idea! It's the least you deserve.'

The four of them stood chatting for a couple of minutes until someone else came to grab Clyde's attention and then they moved on.

She and John drifted into a niche at the edge of the crowd; outside of the crush. 'Right!' declared her boss. 'I estimate that someone will start the inevitable speech in about ten minutes, so I'll get us something to drink first. You stay here, so I'll know where to find you. Back in a trice!'

Jill's eyes searched the crowds, pretending she wasn't looking for Blake. She located him easily. He was taller than most of the men, so it wasn't difficult to pick him out; he was standing on the other side of the room. He was also studying the room calmly. Jill thought she noticed his square jaw tighten when he spotted her. Seeing him again sent her pulses spinning. He regarded her steadily for a moment, and Jill's mind reeled in confusion. He moved in her direction, and a surge of mixed feelings flooded through her. She froze to the spot and waited. There was no point in trying to avoid him, and she didn't honestly want to.

By the time he reached her, she had her emotions better under control. She masked her inner turmoil with an appearance of composure. He was wearing a light grey suit with a conservative shirt and a red tie. She had only ever seen him in casual wear before, but he looked just as good in more formal clothes.

She gave him a tentative smile, and took the lead. 'Hello, Blake!'

A flash of humour crossed his face. 'That's a relief — at least I'm not Mr Armand any more!'

She took a deep breath. 'Yes. Well ... we've both achieved what we wanted. I sold the island, and you've managed to preserve it as a nature reserve. I expect you're delighted that it'll remain a sanctuary, aren't you?'

He was holding a glass of white wine in one hand, and lifted the other to acknowledge someone who called to him from across the room. 'Naturally! It was extraordinarily generous and big-hearted of Chapman to donate the island to the Trust.'

Jill nodded energetically. 'I was really surprised when I heard; it's an astonishing gesture, isn't it? Are there any new plans for it, or will it remain as wild as it is at present?'

He seemed as glad as she was to be holding a normal conversation.

'There's been some talk about using it as a training centre for the area. It would be an ideal place to hold weekend courses, or even for housing people on long-term training. To do so, the house needs to be modernised, but perhaps the board can dig up the funds for that, or ask for specific donations to do so.'

'It wouldn't need to be modernised

in the same way as it would if a family lived there, but some things have to be done to make it habitable.'

His eyes were openly amused. 'Agreed — electricity, new wiring, central heating, perhaps, and then it'll be ready to go!'

'Well . . . some interior decoration to make it a bit more pleasant too, but that doesn't mean professional decoration, I'm sure some enthusiastic helpers could easily paint walls and so on. The furniture is old-fashioned but serviceable and the kitchen will need some basic equipment!'

He grimaced. 'We managed with what was there that night, and survived by just burning wood, didn't we?'

Her colour heightened and her breathing quickened. 'Yes, but that was an emergency. Using wood would mean replenishing supplies constantly, not a very sensible or environmental-friendly prospect! Long-term visitors will have to cook and have somewhere comfortable and warm to sleep.'

'Here we are, my love!' John was back, carrying two glasses of wine. He nodded at Blake, glanced knowingly at Jill's face and said cheerfully, 'Morning! I think you must be Blake Armand? Thought so! I see you already have something to drink? Here's to Coomer Island reserve, then! Cheers!'

Blake lifted his glass. 'I'll drink to that.' He took a gulp and looked around. 'I have to get back; my boss is about to step into the limelight, to accept the gift from Chapman on behalf of the Trust, and I have to be around to cheer him on.'

John nodded understandingly and watched Jill's expression as Blake said in her direction, 'I hope to see you again — sometime soon?'

Her emotions whirled and skidded and she was astonished at the delight she felt. Despite her suddenly dry throat, somehow she managed to sound relaxed. 'Yes, I hope so too.' She added, on impulse, 'Let me know if you'd like me to lend a hand with the painting. I can always fit in a weekend.'

Blake looked pleased. With a nod in John's direction, he merged into the crowd. Someone called for attention and the room prepared for the formal part of the get-together.

'Well, well! For someone who couldn't stand the sight of the man a short time ago you certainly have the knack of wrapping him round your finger, don't you?' John laughed softly and Jill glared at him.

7

A couple of weeks later, the longed-for telephone call came. She silently thanked fate that she had been in the office, and not out with a client.

'Jill? Blake here — we're decorating the bedrooms in the house the weekend after next.' He paused. 'Does your offer of help still stand? Don't hesitate to say no, if you have something else on.'

'No . . . no, I'd be glad to help. I said I would.'

His voice sounded pleased. 'Good! A couple of conservation supporters are ripping the old wallpaper off this weekend and re-papering them. Next weekend we're going to paint them. Are you still game?'

'Yes, of course.'

'Right! Do you have a sleeping bag, in case we miss the tide? You can come whenever you like. The electricity has been reconnected, and the water-pump is working, so it should be a lot more comfortable than the last time we were there.'

'Good! Do you need anything — brushes, buckets, paint?'

'No, all that has been sorted out.'

'And food?'

'The basic stuff for supper and breakfast — bread, cheese, jam, coffee, tea and so on.'

'Can you cook anything in the kitchen?'

'We now have one of those two-hob electric cooker things.'

'That'll do, I'll bring some stuff to fry. How many people will be there?'

There was a short pause. 'Just you and me, like last time.'

Jill had a lump in her throat and she floundered before she managed at last to reply. 'Okay! If you think of something else I can bring, let me know!'

'I will. I'll expect you when I see you.'

Jill held on to the phone tightly and steadied her thoughts.

Time dragged. Jill's sleeping bag dated from her teenage years, so she reasoned it was time she bought a new one. It was lighter, compacter and looked a lot nicer. She wrestled with herself to decide when she should turn up — Friday evening, or Saturday morning. Would it look too eager if she went on Friday evening? In the end, she set out early on Saturday morning.

His car was parked where she expected to find it, and she was able to cross to the island at eight-thirty in the morning without wading through too much water. Her backpack was full, and she held a small holdall aloft to protect it as she made her way towards the jetty. The flow of the tide-water was already rushing and bubbling over her wellingtons as it raced on. The weather was good.

She reached solid ground and made her way quickly along the familiar grass-grown turnings in the pathway.

There was a tingling in her stomach as she thought of seeing Blake again — like an infatuated eighteen-year-old.

As she approached the house, she saw someone had placed an old wooden table, a bench and some broken-down looking chairs outside. There was a pleasant breeze rustling through the undergrowth and an enjoyable scent of sun-kissed grassland, mixed with the salt of the sea. She took a deep breath and looked around. It really was the nicest time of the year. Buttercups and daisies dotted the slope, and there were the sounds and movements of birds everywhere.

As she approached the front door, her nervousness hadn't subsided. It was open, and she went in and dumped her backpack. Laurence barked and came pounding down the stairs, claws clattering on the floor. He jumped up, covered her face with kisses, wagging his tail furiously.

She took his silky head in her hands. 'Hello, my friend!'

Movement at the top of the stairs compelled her to look up. Blake stood there, tough, lean and sinewy, in a pair of washed-out jeans and a red and black check shirt, and her eyes froze on his form.

As casually as she could manage, she said, 'Hi, Blake!'

His voice echoed the warmth of his smile. 'At last! I thought I'd be doing it all on my own!'

'A promise is a promise!'

He gave her another smile that did nothing to calm her racing pulse. 'Why don't you make some coffee and I'll come down for a break.'

'What about working?'

'There's plenty to do up here, but there's a time and a place for everything.'

'Okay. I'll call you.'

He nodded and turned away. Jill was glad of a few minutes on her own to adjust. She made the coffee and unpacked some biscuits. Laurence eyed her wistfully and she gave him one.

When she was ready, she called Blake and carried everything outside. Laurence followed and found himself a spot in the sun. The clatter of feet on the stairs announced Blake's imminent arrival and he threw himself into one of the ramshackle chairs. It wobbled and then righted itself. He leaned back contentedly and turned his face to the sun. Jill noticed a couple of paint spots on his cheek. She thought about telling him — and offering to remove them — but she said and did nothing.

'Mm! This is good! Have a safe journey?'

'No problems. How long have you been here?'

'Since last night.' Jill kicked herself that she hadn't come earlier. 'The group finished the wallpapering last week, and I started on one of the small bedrooms yesterday evening before daylight faded. I'm almost finished.'

'What colour?'

He laughed softly. 'Trust a woman to ask. Off-white — everyone thought that was the best idea.'

'It is. It can always be painted another colour later on! What about the other jobs like central heating and rewiring?'

He grabbed some biscuits. 'The wiring is finished, didn't you notice? There are long slits in the walls everywhere downstairs. They've been more or less plastered over everywhere. Upstairs they're already under the wallpaper, but downstairs they're still visible.'

She took a sip of coffee and pushed the plate of biscuits towards him. 'No, I didn't notice. So we now have electricity?'

'Yes. Electricity and water, and an electric boiler in the bathroom!'

'What luxury!'

'There's still discussion about how to heat the place properly. Using electricity would be very expensive unless we can negotiate for special tariffs for night storage heaters. We're using portable radiant heaters at the moment.'

'That's luxurious in comparison to heating the place with the stove in the living room and the Rayburn in the kitchen — if that still functions.'

Blake scratched his forehead. 'We're getting someone in to check that, before we use it. I have no idea if it can be converted to some other kind of fuel. As you said, burning wood on an island is not environmentally friendly!'

'What do you want me to do?'

'I thought you could paint the other small bedroom. I'll do the double bedroom.'

'If they put bunk beds in the bedrooms, you'll double the sleeping capacity. People on weekend courses won't expect luxury. If it's used in long-term training, you wouldn't have so many people staying here at one time, and it wouldn't matter if all of the bunk beds aren't in constant use.'

'That's not a bad idea! I'll pass it on.'

'Oh — and I suppose I'll need a paint roller, won't I? Got any spares?'

He nodded. 'There are a couple in

the hallway in plastic bags, and some long-handled brushes, so you should be okay. I borrowed from some friends.' He paused and his grey eyes covered her face. 'By the way, how are you? Busy — in work?'

'I'm fine. Plenty to do in the office, but no panic. Luckily John is a very laid-back boss.'

'Good!' He surveyed the remains of the gardens and looked towards the sea thoughtfully. 'It's a bit of a shame to work in this good weather, but if we finish early enough, we might just have enough time to enjoy the island.' He tipped his head in the direction of the untamed regions of the slope in front of the house.' I was thinking yesterday that it might not be a bad idea to keep some of the area around the house tamed. There's bags of room for the animals and birds. If the house does become a training centre, it would be sensible to have some free space.'

She followed his glance. 'Yes, I think so, too. The path to the jetty needs cutting back too, doesn't it? It's growing wild. If people have to fight their way through every time, it won't be much fun.'

He nodded. Her attention wandered to how strongly his fingers encompassed the mug. 'Have you done any more walking?'

'No, I keep thinking about it, but you know how it is — and I need a friend who'll go with me. I didn't think it would be sensible to walk any distances in open countryside unless I had company.'

'Agreed! An important safety aspect, especially for any woman. If you like, and haven't found a willing friend before then, you're invited to come with me, on my next walk. I don't know where to, but as long as you just want to walk and enjoy the countryside, I don't suppose you mind, do you?'

'Er — no! I'd like that.'

'Good; I'll let you know where and when.' He drank the last dregs of coffee and absentmindedly ate a couple more biscuits. He got up and stretched. Jill mused that he seemed to touch the sky. 'Well, I suppose I'd better get back to work, otherwise I'll never finish.'

She stood up. 'Yes, after I've changed, I'll join you.'

★   ★   ★

Jill stood back and studied the finished walls. Adding a few brushstrokes here and there, she felt quite satisfied with the results. She looked at her watch and was surprised how quickly time had passed. She'd almost forgotten that Blake was working in the next room. Looking round the doorframe, she could see he was almost finished too.

He looked back and gave her a crooked smile. She felt a warm glow flow through her. She was slowly accepting the fact that Blake Armand had an effect on her that she'd never experienced with any man before. Just a glance from him and her body seemed to turn to liquid.

She cleared her throat. 'I've finished. Would you like me to help you? If not, I'll clean up the mess in the finished rooms. What do we do with the paintbrushes? We can't wash them out here, can we?'

He shook his head. Jill noticed that a couple more blobs of paint had joined those on his face. 'No, I've brought a pile of plastic bags — downstairs in the kitchen. Put the brushes in them and tape them — when I get them home I'll wash them out.' He bent to fill the roller with paint again. 'Carry on doing what you like! Sit in the sun, if you want to.' He looked at his watch. 'I should be finished in an hour or so.'

'Okay!' She looked around. 'It looks good. Amazing what fresh paint can do, and the light colour brings a lot more brightness into the room, doesn't it?' She disappeared and clattered down stairs again. Laurence was glad of the interruption and followed her. She opened the door and he went out gratefully, sniffing the ground and lifting his wet nose to the breezes dancing round the house. Jill left him there, and went to look for the plastic bags and a bucket to do a bit of basic cleaning.

Some time later she stood back and viewed a clean-looking, clean-smelling, freshly painted room. She'd even managed to remove the grime from the windows. She attacked the other small bedroom, listening with one ear to the movements from the neighbouring room. Sometimes she heard him whistling softly, and it made her feel good.

Jill didn't particularly like housework, but by the time she had attacked the bathroom, she felt quite pleased with herself. She jumped a little when his voice floated over her shoulder.

'Good Lord! If ever I'm looking for a charlady, I'll know where to come. I don't suppose it's looked this clean since the last owner moved out!'

Jill grinned at him. 'If something hasn't been cleaned for a long time, the difference is very noticeable. Have you finished? If so, I may as well clean your bedroom too — and then the upstairs is practically finished. With new mattresses, and a bit of polish on the furniture, the rooms will already be quite habitable!'

His eyes twinkled and his mouth widened in approval. 'Perhaps we'll find someone to make us some simple bunk-beds at some stage. I didn't reckon on you cleaning as well. Thanks! You've helped a lot in such a short time.'

'I was glad to help, honestly!'

He eyed her thoughtfully. 'Who'd believe that an elegant creature like you would be so down-to-earth and practical?'

She flushed with pleasure. 'I'm a farmer's daughter — remember? There's always work to be done on a farm, and everyone mucks in.'

Blake nodded. 'If you really insist on cleaning this room, I'll help! I'll do the floor and you do whatever else you think should be done.'

'Can you? Men sometimes don't know one end of the scrubbing brush from the other!'

'Well I do! It comes from my living on my own. Either you give in and only do what's necessary to survive, or learn to be clean. I don't enjoy cleaning, but I do see the necessity — from time to time!'

She laughed. 'Okay! I believe you. Here's the bucket and floor cloth; I'll go and find some other container I can use for cleaning the windows.'

Laurence was lying in the doorway, his head on his paws. She stroked him in passing on her way to the garden shed. Her search was rewarded with a battered but watertight plastic bowl, and with washing-up liquid and the roll of kitchen paper under her arm, she joined him again. In companionable silence, they each concentrated on their chosen task.

Leaning on the mop, he looked around when they were finished. 'Great! Thanks Jill! Together, we've done a good job.'

His praise was all she wanted. 'I

think so too. When are improvements planned for the downstairs rooms?'

'Oh, the wiring has to be plastered over properly yet, and they're fixing a second-hand cooker and a fridge in the kitchen soon, but nothing has been finally settled yet. I think someone has offered cheap radiant gas heaters for the bedrooms. Anyway, we've done enough for one day. Let's get cleaned up and get something to eat, I'm starving!'

'I've brought sandwiches and some other food.' She looked out of the window. 'It's really pleasant out there. Shall we go down to the cove and have a picnic?'

'A good idea! In fact I can't wait until we are cleaned up. I don't know about you but once I've washed my hands, I'll be ready to go.'

'Right! Then let's go!'

The golden light of the late afternoon sun was everywhere. The waves swished and gurgled and the breezes blowing in from the water were pleasant. The air was cool and sweet and very pure; heady with the smell of the salt water and the island's plant life. She unpacked the food and they sat companionably next to each other on the rocks in contentment.

Munching on a moist sandwich, she touched the corner of her mouth with a finger and asked, 'Have you seen any more seals?'

Blake shook his head. 'I'm sure that they're around here all the time, but I haven't been back here much since Clyde officially gave it to the Trust.' He reached out for a sausage roll and proceeded to enjoy it. The pastry crumbled and bits of it were carried off by the wind.

'Will you be responsible for the island?'

He shrugged and brushed the flakes from his hands. 'It depends on its eventual use. If it does end up as a main training centre, probably not, but I won't mind if that happens.'

He stretched and crossed his hands behind his head.

The sun caught his face, and the

paint spots were even more discernible against his tanned skin. Her eyes twinkled and she grinned. 'Do you realise you're covered in paint?'

He turned to look at her in mock horror. 'Really? Am I indeed? Where?'

Jill reached forward and touched his face with a finger. His gaze travelled over her and searched her eyes. Her heart jolted and her pulse pounded. Her whole being was filled with waiting for this moment; the smouldering flame in his eyes startled her. He leaned towards her and she felt his lips touch her like a whisper. She kissed him back with a hunger that belied her previous outward calm. The gentle power of his kiss left her weak, and she was startled by her own response. She had known there was something special about him from the very beginning and she'd tried to ignore it — but it had only taken one kiss to realise just how special he was to her.

Softly his breath fanned her cheek as he murmured, 'I've been wanting to do that for a very long time.'

'Have you?' She found the thought very satisfying.

His arms encircled her and reclaimed her. Another kiss sent new spirals of delight through her, and she returned it with reckless abandon. When they parted momentarily, his face split into a wide grin and, borne on a wave of sheer joy, she rewarded him with a smile just as large.

The sound of Laurence's bark startled them and they drew apart. Someone was approaching. Jill's heart was still hammering wildly and her breathing was ragged when she spotted Sharon Burton coming down the slope from the house. Her heart sank when she saw Sharon lift her hand to wave; her appearance foreshadowed a feeling of disappointment and apprehension. What was she doing here? Jill shut her eyes for a moment. Blake stood up and shoved his hands in his pockets to face Sharon as she approached.

Reaching them, Sharon said cheerily.

'Hi you two! I heard you were here today. I thought I'd come to help.'

Jill wondered if Sharon had seen them kissing. If so, she hid it with ease.

Sharon moved to Blake's side. 'Can't let my favourite boyfriend down, and not rally round if he needs support, can I?'

Blake's voice was cool but he didn't correct her in any way. 'Only trouble is, you always manage to turn up when someone else has done the work, Sharon — or haven't you noticed?'

A chill hung on the edge of her words but her laughed tinkled, and she placed her hand possessively on his arm. 'Not intended, pet! I couldn't get here earlier. All a matter of fate and bad timing, I expect.' She glanced briefly at the remains of their picnic. 'If you're finished here, you can show me the results of your work? Jill was obviously here to be your willing slave, so you have nothing to complain about.' Finally, she managed to say condescendingly, 'Hi Jill! How are you?'

Jill's breath burned in her throat. 'Hi, there, Sharon. I'm fine, thanks!'

Blake's voice was smooth and insistent. 'How did you get here?'

She replied hastily, 'Look at the time, darling! The tide was just right, and I came across by foot. Show me the house. I've never been here. It would be a cosy place to spend the night. Quite romantic, I imagine.'

It was clear that Sharon had come to stay; she did not intend to leave again as long as Blake was around. Jill was struggling with unanswered questions that were lingering on the edges of her mind. She forced her swirling emotions into order and waited while adjusting to the new situation.

Sharon tugged at Blake's sleeve, demanding his attention again. 'Show me this house, and what you've been doing all day.'

Blake half-turned and looked at Jill with an unspoken message as they climbed the slope. Jill looked down at the shingles at her feet. All the pleasure had gone out of the day.

Sharon was chatting, nineteen to the dozen. Jill wondered if she was more to Blake than just a casual friend. The way she acted and the way he responded raised doubts in her.

Perhaps Blake had only kissed her spontaneously without intending any involvement or implied infatuation; perhaps he was just flirting with her and she meant nothing to him. Jill knew now that she was helplessly in love with him, and vulnerable because of it. She hated the idea that he might be in love with someone else — but it was possible. Until their kiss just now, he'd never really singled her out, she thought.

Packing up the remains of their picnic and taking a deep breath to steady her nerves, Jill followed them up the slope and into the house. She listened to their voices as they wandered around the upstairs rooms and she braced herself. She re-packed the rest of her things quickly. Sharon was here to stay. She wouldn't leave Blake alone with Jill. Perhaps Sharon had prior claims to him; perhaps not, but Jill didn't intend to spend any heart-rending time finding out exactly what the situation between them was. She would feel so humiliated if he'd only being playing with her emotions. If she didn't cross to the mainland soon, before the tide turned again, she'd be stuck here with them for another eight hours. She hoisted her backpack and picked up her holdall.

Calling up the stairs, she managed to sound calm. 'I'm off now! Bye!'

There was a scuffle of feet above, but Jill was already on her way out. She heard raised voices, but hurried through the undergrowth, almost at a run, and strode across the wet shingle as if walking on hot coals. She didn't look back. Tears found their way down her cheeks as she stuffed her things in the boot of her car, got in, and drove off feeling more miserable than she'd ever felt in her life before.

8

In spite of Jill's busy schedule, thoughts of Blake kept intruding into her day. She had appointments all morning with various clients. After lunch, she returned to the office. Not even John noticed her usually sparkling eyes were dull and lifeless. She unpacked her briefcase and started to sort out the various papers. She gave up trying, and sat in her chair with her slim fingers tensed in her lap, her eyes on the window, and her thoughts still circling Saturday's events.

Clive knocked, came in, and gave an anxious cough when she made no response. 'That chap phoned again. I had trouble getting rid of him. He was almost offensive when I insisted you weren't there and would be out all morning. I just kept on refusing and in the end, he hung up. I . . . I hope I did the right thing?'

'Yes, of course.' Jill was still deep in her own thoughts and only registered his words vaguely. She wakened from her trance and asked, 'What man?'

'The one you wanted me to put off before — a while back.'

'You mean Blake Armand?'

'Yes, that was the name — Blake Armand.'

Her pale face grew paler; then she just leaned back and sighed. What did it matter? He didn't feel anything special for her; so why worry?

'That's all right, Clive. Thanks!'

Clive went out, relieved that he hadn't put his foot in it.

★   ★   ★

Next morning Jill was busy opening her post. One envelope caught her eye. Her name and address were handwritten, in bold black ink. She slit it and took out the matching sheet of paper. A glance at the signature sent the colour to her cheeks.

Dear Jill,

I tried to contact you yesterday, but someone blocked my attempts. I have to go away on business until Friday, that's why I'm writing (I don't have your private address or telephone number). You rushed off on Saturday without giving me the chance to say thank you, or to give you details about that walk I was planning. How about this Saturday, starting roughly ten o'clock, from the visitors' centre? Don't disappoint me — you said you never break a promise. I look forward to seeing you, very much.

Blake

Jill read it through twice, and then crumpled it into a ball and threw it into the bin. She hadn't promised him anything; she'd only said she'd *like* to go on his next walk. A possibility wasn't a promise! She had no wish to be one of a crowd trailing after him all day like last time — and Sharon might be there too, hanging on his arm.

She tried to dismiss his letter, but it gnawed away inside like a painful wound. She was preoccupied with her thoughts and often caught herself staring vacantly out of the window.

It came to a head two days later when John marched into her room with a sheaf of papers in his hand.

'Poppet, what is going on? You've just given me the contract for Thomas, but you've filled it with the details for the people who bought the terraced house in Wilmot Street! Are you feeling ill? You never usually make this sort of mistake.'

Jill looked up at him, gulped hard, before hot tears began to slip down her cheeks.

'So, there — drink your tea, and tell me what's up!'

Jill did, and like a good friend, John listened without commenting.

'He may be two-timing his steady girlfriend. Perhaps he's just being friendly and I'm interpreting too much into the whole thing.' She took a tissue from the box he held out towards her, and blew her nose.

John sat on the corner of the desk and gazed at her. 'Well, you may be unsure about what he feels, but you've decided about how you feel. You've fallen for him, haven't you?'

Jill crumpled the paper hanky in her hands, looked down and nodded.

'I think so!'

'Well, for what it's worth, I think that you should pluck up courage and go on Saturday. What have you got to lose? If this other woman is there, at least you'll get a chance to see how involved he is. He can't spend a whole day with this woman and ignore her if she is his girlfriend, can he? If he is involved, it might not be fun to watch, but at least you'll find out where you stand. You have to be honest; some people might be satisfied with sharing, but you're not one of those. In the long run it will be better to accept that he's not for you, than to live with uncertainty or even a lie — even if it hurts!'

Jill nodded.

'Here.' He handed her his beautifully ironed, folded white handkerchief. 'Take the rest of the day off. Go out and buy yourself a pair of shoes, or whatever women do to cheer themselves up. You're not much use to me in the office today.'

She got up and kissed him on the cheek. 'Thanks, John. I'll be all right tomorrow, I promise. I'll go through everything I've done this week, make sure I've not made any other stupid mistakes.' She gave him a shaky smile.

'That's my girl! Off you go; and there's a pair of snakeskin shoes in Blundle's window that are absolutely fabulous!'

★　★　★

Saturday dawned. Jill had been awake for ages. A glance out of the window told her it was going to be a day full of sunshine. She looked at her resolute

175

face in the mirror and brushed neatness back into her hair.

By the time she got to the visitors' centre, the sun was already shining from a cloudless sky. She left her Mini in the car park and walked along the lane where there was nothing but the trees and bushes lining the way, and some birds chirping in the undergrowth. She hoisted her backpack to a more comfortable position when the roof of the centre came into view. She looked at her watch and saw she was early, but she was still surprised to see no one else hanging around outside. There was no reason for her to go inside — the meeting place was out here, so she stood and waited.

She looked up when the door opened. Blake shut it with a loud thud. A backpack hung loosely from his hand and he seemed very pleased with himself. His good looks totally captured her attention.

She took a steadying breath, feeling a

lurch of excitement inside her. 'Morning, Blake! Isn't it a lovely day?'

He clattered down the steps and glanced up at the sky briefly. 'Perfect!' He smiled. 'So . . . are you ready?'

Jill glanced around. 'I am, but where are the others?'

He looked puzzled. 'Others? What do you mean, others?'

'The other people coming on the walk.'

'There are no others, it's just you and me. I never said anyone else was coming, did I?'

She swallowed hard. 'No one else?'

'No, apart from Laurence.' He whistled and the black dog appeared out of nowhere.

Laurence immediately began to show his obvious pleasure at seeing her again, and Jill was glad of the diversion to get her thoughts back in order.

'Laurence took to you from the very first day, didn't he?' commented Blake thoughtfully.

Jill buried her face in the dog's fur to

give herself time to compose herself. 'He's just a friendly dog. Anyone who fusses over him ends up being his friend!'

Blake laughed softly. 'Perhaps, but there are all kinds of friendships, aren't there? Some friendships last a lifetime! Shall we go? I have a feeling that some of the staff in there are watching us with interest.'

Jill coloured slightly. 'Are they? Why? Where are we going?'

He tucked his arm through hers and directed her towards the lane and the woodland they'd gone through last time Jill had been on a walking tour with him. He began to chuckle.

'What's the matter?'

'Oh nothing! I'm just thinking about the remarks someone just dropped in the centre.'

'What about?' There was no way she could extract her arm without making an issue out of it, so Jill left it where it was.

'You, of course!'

'Me? They don't know me.'

'Perhaps not, but they've never known their boss to go on a walk with one special girl. That's giving them plenty of food for thought.'

They'd reached the covering greenery of the woodland. There was an aroma of grasses in the air and the sunlight rippled through the branches. Jill felt there was nothing else in the world — only Blake, the trees, and a diffused green light all around.

All at once he came to an abrupt halt and turned her towards him. Somewhere nearby a stream bubbled and rushed on its way.

Holding her firmly within his embrace, his mouth covered hers hungrily and a shockwave went through her body. It was a kiss to fire her soul, and when it was over she breathed lightly between parted lips as she looked up at his handsome face. She felt the defences she'd built up since she last saw him crumbling away.

He bent his head towards her again

and she put up her hand to cover his mouth. She knew she'd be lost forever if she didn't sort her misgivings out straight away.

Breathlessly, she said, 'Blake, you know I'm not someone who believes in playing around.'

He gave her a crooked smile, looking longingly at her lips. 'No, I didn't think you were.'

'What about Sharon?'

He looked at her, puzzled. 'I don't know. What do you mean by that?'

She swallowed a lump in her throat. 'Is she your steady girlfriend — perhaps even more — or not?'

He looked at her in surprise and then threw back his head to laugh. It echoed among the trees. 'Sharon? My girl-friend? What gave you that idea?'

Determinedly she ploughed on, as the colour in her face heightened. 'She always gave me the distinct impression that she was someone special in your life.'

He touched the side of her jaw with

one finger and looked thoughtful. 'You're sweet, do you know that? If she gave you that impression, then it was a false one! Sharon is good at her job — even if she didn't handle your fear of heights properly. I have a lot to do with her because the people at the activity centre and the conservation people have to work hand in hand, but that's as far as it goes between us.'

He fenced with the words for a moment, but then he continued. 'I'd be stupid not to admit I notice she seems to have developed some kind of obsession about me, but I've never encouraged her. I've even told her I'm not interested in so many words, but it doesn't seem to make any difference. Her attention is annoying and embarrassing.'

He paused and studied her, dropping his arms to run his hands through his hair. 'I wish you hadn't run off like that on Saturday. I wondered if you'd got the wrong impression. Drat the woman! Sharon's appearance threw me, because

I never reckoned with her turning up. I don't know how she found out I was on Coomer — probably the people at the visitors' centre. There was I, feeling happy that we were on our own at last, and then she butted in.'

'She was demonstratively possessive, and made me believe that you were much more than friends.'

'Jill, what could I do, short of throwing her off the island into the channel? I honestly thought we'd be able to make her understand we expected her to leave before the tide came in properly — after a very short visit. My wish was for us to be on our own — to spend the night there, if you agreed.'

Jill swallowed a lump in her throat. He continued.

'You ran off like a scalded cat, and were out of reach before I realised what had happened. I didn't stay on the island either after that. I gathered everything together and bundled us over onto the mainland in my boat. I sent Sharon on her way with a flea in her ear. I was furious at her, and told her I never wanted to see her again unless there was a professional reason. I said she should stay out of my private life now because I'd met someone whom I love — someone who I hope wants me as much as I want her.'

He gazed at Jill and there was fire in his eyes. Hope began to blossom inside her.

'I would have come after you on Saturday, but I didn't have your telephone number, or your address, so I couldn't. I couldn't out-trick your guard dog in the office either, so writing was the only way I had left. I had to go up to London, and I just prayed that you'd give me the chance today to be alone with you, to try to convince you how much you mean to me.'

She nodded silently. He gripped her shoulders again. 'I love you! I've never felt like this before. I've never been so certain, so sure. You're the part of me that's always been missing. I can't imagine living without you. Do I have a chance?'

At last Jill felt she could be truthful, with him and with herself. She raised her eyes and met his gaze.

'You have the best chance — the only chance anyone will ever have, Blake — I love you too.'

A smile spread across his face and his eyes sparkled. He pulled her closer, easing her backpack from her shoulders so that it fell to the ground, and kissed her again, longingly and searchingly.

When he could speak once more he said huskily, 'I fell in love with you the moment I found you, all spread out on the rock — the first time you went to Coomer Island. You reminded me of the fairytale about the Little Mermaid, with your green eyes and blonde hair. You were, and you are, my enchantress!'

She tapped his nose playfully. 'Ah, but that story didn't have a happy end — the prince married someone else.'

He chuckled. 'Did he? I only said you

reminded me of a mermaid, I didn't say our story is going to be the same. Heaven forbid!'

'I hope you understood why I got angry at you when you barged in on my meeting with Clyde? I knew you were trying to save the island, but I didn't like you interfering.'

He nodded wordlessly, and drew her into his arms for another satisfactory kiss. He cupped her face in his hands. 'I love my work, and sometimes I get carried away. I'm afraid that will never change. Can you live with that?'

She nodded and turned her head to kiss one of his palms. She felt at peace with the world and immensely happy. She could leave the future to take care of itself. Blake and she had plenty of time now to find out whether they were meant for each other. Doubts and obstacles had been removed.

With shining eyes, they kissed again. Then Blake helped her lift her backpack, and tucked his arm through hers once more. Laurence circled them, barking his approval.

'I think this is going to be one of the best walks I've ever undertaken.'

* * *

Jill's mother held the phone receiver away from her ear and looked at it in exaggerated puzzlement. 'I know that I've been dropping hints about boy-friends and a lasting relationship, love — but don't you think it is a bit early in the year to make plans about bringing someone home for Christmas? Perhaps you won't still be with him by then!'

'Mum! I'm not talking about bring-ing Blake home for Christmas, I want to bring him home as soon as possible. I'm going to be with him forever more, so you may as well get used to him, and I think it would be an excellent idea for everyone to meet him before we get engaged, don't you?'

The breath left her mother's lungs for a moment. 'Engaged? Blake is the young man you've mentioned so often in the last couple of weeks? How wonderful. He must be a very special man to have knocked you off your feet so quickly.'

'Oh, he is. Definitely. He's the very, very best. And I know that you're all going to like him.'

THE END

TAKE MY BREATH AWAY

Beth James

After the failure of her first marriage, romantic writer Emma has built a sheltered, secure life for herself and her four-year-old daughter. The last thing she needs on the horizon is a handsome stranger with an attractive smile. To make matters worse, her roof is leaking, money is tight and her ex-husband is taking a renewed interest in her life. Suddenly, Emma finds herself with as many complications to deal with as the tempestuous heroines in her romantic novels.

ALL ABOUT ADAM

Moyra Tarling

Teacher Paris Ford hopes to improve the performances of Brockton College's basketball team. But going to the new athletic director for help, she's confronted by the startlingly handsome Adam Kincaid. Years ago, Paris secretly witnessed Adam's role in her family's scandal and she isn't about to forgive or forget. However, Adam's tender kisses melt her resolve to maintain a professional relationship. Now she must discover the truth about Adam's past and look toward a future . . . with the man she loved.

NASHVILLE CINDERELLA

Julia Douglas

In Nashville, thousands of talented people hope to make the big time ... Starstruck Cindy Coin came from Alabama, but still works in Lulu's diner, alongside Tony — who's yet to make his mark. Hank Donno, looking every inch the successful manager, hopes to find his big star — then wide-eyed Katie arrives. And travelling on the Greyhound, Texan Jack just hopes that Nashville is ready for him. Can hopes and dreams be realised? And is romance in the air in Nashville?

MY TRUE COMPANION

Sally Quilford

It is 1921. Social pariah Millie Woodridge is obliged to obtain employment as a companion for ageing actress, Mrs Oakengate, when her father is unjustly executed on charges of espionage. During a weekend house party Millie meets handsome adventurer, James Haxby, and is soon drawn into the dark, but thrilling world of espionage. Unsure who to trust, Millie joins James in tracking down a callous murderer and uncovering the truth about her father.

CHERISH THE DREAM

Teresa Ashby

Darcie Westbrook is determined not to let herself be hurt by another man, but she can't help falling for vet Glenn Hunter who is a regular visitor at her animal sanctuary. A property developer is out to take her land and build a housing estate on it, and someone is attacking horses. It is only when Glenn's life is in danger, as he fights to protect the horses, that Darcy admits her true feelings for him.

EARL GRESHAM'S BRIDE

Angela Drake

When heiress Kate Roscoe compromises herself through an innocent mistake, widower, Earl Gresham steps in with an offer of marriage to save her reputation. She is soon deeply in love with him, but is beset by the problems of overseeing his grand household. The housekeeper is dishonest and the nanny of the earl's two children is heartless and lazy. But a far greater threat comes from his former mistress who will go to any lengths to destroy Kate's marriage.